# Mr. Tough Guy had been weakened by a little fluffy dog.

Emily pressed her lips together so as not to laugh. "We have dog obedience classes here a couple of nights a week." She handed him a pamphlet.

"Do you teach these classes?"

"I mainly run the office, but I also own a dog-sitting and dog-walking business." She hadn't meant to tell him that, but it was too late now. He needed to learn to take care of his own animals.

"I—I might like to use your dog-walking service if you could fit me in."

"I'm filled up right now."

"I'd still like your card if you have one. You never know."

She knew. She could handle dogs, but she couldn't handle Martin Davis. She dug into her pocket, pulled out a card and handed it to him.

"Thanks. Will you call me if you get an opening?"

Emily forced herself to be firm. "My customers stay with me a long time." When she looked at his expression, she wished she'd been gentler.

He didn't look back as he marched outside. Apparently Martin wasn't a man to accept the word *no*.

**Books by Gail Gaymer Martin**

Love Inspired

*Loving Treasures
*Loving Hearts
Easter Blessings
  "The Butterfly Garden"
The Harvest
  "All Good Gifts"
*Loving Ways
*Loving Care
Adam's Promise
*Loving Promises
*Loving Feelings

*Loving Tenderness
**In His Eyes
**With Christmas in His Heart
**In His Dreams
**Family in His Heart
Dad in Training
Groom in Training
Bride in Training

*Loving
**Michigan Islands

Steeple Hill Books

The Christmas Kite
Finding Christmas

That Christmas Feeling
  "Christmas Moon"

## GAIL GAYMER MARTIN

A former counselor, Gail Gaymer Martin is an award-winning author of women's fiction, romance and romantic suspense. *Bride in Training* is her forty-third published work of long fiction; she has three million books in print. Gail is the author of twenty-five worship resource books and also wrote the book *Writing the Christian Romance* released by Writer's Digest Books. She is a cofounder of American Christian Fiction Writers, the premier Christian fiction organization in the country.

When not behind her computer, Gail enjoys a busy life—traveling, presenting workshops at conferences, speaking at churches and libraries, and singing as a soloist, praise leader and choir member at her church, where she also plays handbells and hand chimes. She also sings with one of the finest Christian chorales in Michigan, the Detroit Lutheran Singers. Gail is a lifelong resident of Michigan and lives with her husband, Bob, in the Detroit suburbs. To learn more about her, visit her Web site at www.gailmartin.com. Write to Gail at P.O. Box 760063, Lathrup Village, MI 48076, or at authorgailmartin@aol.com. She enjoys hearing from readers.

# Bride in Training
## Gail Gaymer Martin

Steeple
Hill®

Published by Steeple Hill Books™

STEEPLE HILL BOOKS

Steeple Hill®

Recycling programs for this product may not exist in your area.

ISBN-13: 978-0-373-87612-9

BRIDE IN TRAINING

Copyright © 2010 by Gail Gaymer Martin

www.SteepleHill.com

**Printed in U.S.A.**

By his mighty power at work within us,
he is able to accomplish infinitely more than
we would ever dare to ask or hope.
—*Ephesians* 3:20

In memory of our daughter, Brenda Martin Bailey, who lost her life to ovarian cancer in 2006.

And to men and women everywhere who love dogs and provide them with loving homes. From those unions, families receive a blessing, unconditional love, which is an underlying theme in the three novels of the Man's Best Friend series.

# Chapter One

Good decision? Bad?

Martin Davis gripped his steering wheel as he eyed the shelter's Time For Paws neon sign glowing in the dusk. He'd never thought he would darken the doors of a dog shelter, but here he was. Now the question hung in his mind. Was it a good decision or bad one? He'd become lonely without Suzette, his Bouvier, but he hadn't been able to handle her. Sometimes he wondered what he could handle. Not dogs or women, apparently.

So if he couldn't deal with Suzette, why come here to look for another dog? He released his grip on the steering wheel, fell back against the seat, and rubbed his temples. Because he couldn't bear coming home to an empty house any longer. He'd been a failure as a husband. Cats were too aloof. Dogs? He had hopes.

Martin ran his fingers through his hair. He'd been alone for eight years since his wife walked out on him. The loneliness had faded, he thought, but since his brother, Nick, married, he had stopped popping by for visits. That was the whole of it. Being alone wasn't for Martin anymore.

He turned the thought over in his mind. He recalled

Steph and Nick talking about the unconditional love a dog provided. He'd never been one to worry about love or the lack of it, but unconditional love meant someone would be excited to greet him when he came home. A dog's happy yips and wagging tail filled the bill, and a dog wouldn't care if he were preoccupied with his business or even a little edgy at times.

Unconditional love. He shook his head. He sounded like a poet or a psychiatrist. The thought rallied an uneasy grin. Martin turned off the ignition and pushed open the door. If nothing more, he could take a look.

He slipped out of his car and gazed at the gray concrete building, once his friend Brent Runyan's unoccupied factory until Molly wheedled away his building and his heart. They'd married, too. Everyone had gotten tangled in that web of "two by two." He wondered if Noah had any idea what he started when he filled that ark.

Drawing up his shoulders, he headed for the door. The bell jingled as he stepped inside, and in the distance he heard dogs making a ruckus. He glanced at his watch. Dinner time, he guessed. His own stomach gave a rumble.

No one stood behind the desk. He waited, his impatience growing each second. He tapped his foot, staring at the doorway. Maybe this was a dumb decision. It could be God's way of telling him to go home. But maybe not. It might just be bad customer service. Or his impatience. If he asked Nick, that's what his brother would tell him. He had no patience.

Frustrated, he returned to the entrance and swung the door open and closed. The small bell jingled again. With no response, he walked deeper into the room and aimed his gaze at the door standing ajar. Through the opening, he could see a young woman at the far end of a long aisle, but before he could call to her, she turned and headed his way. Her dark hair brushed against her shoulders, her arms swinging past her trim hips as if she had nothing better to do. But he did.

Finally she noticed him and picked up her stride. When she came through the door, the woman paused, a look of curiosity on her face. "Sorry, I hope I didn't keep you waiting too long."

About five minutes came to mind, but Martin didn't offer one of his biting comments. Instead he wondered why she gave him that questioning look.

She stepped closer. "What can I do for you?"

He motioned to the door. "You might change that bell to a siren." Okay, so he'd let that comment sneak out.

"Great idea. Now what can I do for you as far as our dogs are concerned."

Martin noted the sarcasm in her voice, but with it, the flicker of a grin.

The grin faded as she studied him. "I think I know you."

A frown burrowed onto his face.

"I don't really know you, but I've seen you." Her probing gaze raked across his face.

Martin's eyebrow tugged upward.

She gave a knowing nod. "At Steph's wedding. You're Martin Davis, right? Nick's brother."

That explained the look. "Yes, the infamous Martin Davis."

She didn't blink. "I'm Emily Ireland."

Martin eyed her slender hand reaching toward his. He grasped it, surprised her grip was stronger than he'd expected. He gazed into her eyes. Beautiful eyes, wide-set and the color of dark chocolate. Her straight dark brows lifted at the ends, giving her an impish look that caught him off guard. His mind snapped back, and he mumbled a nice-to-meet-you comment, although he wasn't really sure if that would prove to be true. For all her innocence, she made him feel on edge.

Emily released his grip with a new expression more confounding than the last. "Don't tell me you're looking for another dog?"

Ah-ha. She had all the dirt on him from Steph, naturally. "Is that a problem?"

Her uneasiness deepened. "No. It's…it's good."

Martin figured she was trying to make up for her earlier comment. He watched her squirm a little and rub her palms together as if trying to decide what to say or do next.

Martin shoved his hand into his pants pocket unable to understand why looking at her left him confused. Worse than confused. He wanted to give her a hug and suggest they start over, but it would ruin his apparent reputation. "I want a dog, but definitely one quieter and less work than Suzette. I'm sure you've heard about those problems."

She flashed him an uneasy look. "Yes. You gave her to your brother."

Martin's brows knitted, sensing an undertone from this impish woman. "Suzette was rambunctious." Her knowing gaze tripped his pulse.

"Dogs are until they're trained."

Her knowledge of him crept under his skin, and he itched to know more about her. She had the upper hand, and he didn't like it. Maybe he could grill Nick. But subtly. If not, Nick would be all over him to know why he was asking about a Time for Paws employee.

Her demeanor softened, and Emily motioned toward the doorway. "I think I know the perfect dog for you."

Martin arched his brow, curious why this dog was so perfect. Probably it was old and three-legged.

Emily didn't let his look slow her down. She pointed again. "Through that doorway."

He headed for the door, giving up on trying to understand the subliminal feelings charging through him.

Emily moved ahead, her hair brushing against her baggy shirt. Hidden beneath, he sensed, was a woman who was hiding something. Her look was direct, but the flicker behind her intriguing eyes made him wonder. If he asked Steph, she'd be on him like a bloodhound.

As soon as Emily opened the door, a din of woofs and whines rose to greet them. Martin strode past her, glancing inside the pens as tails wagged and noses pressed against the wire fencing of the upper door while the shorter dogs leaped to see above the Dutch door's solid bottom. Martin paused and took a good look at the inside of the pen. "The dogs have furniture. That's odd."

Her demeanor changed and took on a businesslike manner that let him know she'd been offended by his comment. "Coming here is traumatic enough for them, so we try to make the dogs as comfortable as possible."

"Apparently." He didn't let her browbeat him.

"The dog I have in mind is down here." She strutted ahead, her attitude decisive.

Martin followed her down the aisle, gazing into the dog pens. When she reached her destination, a tender look filled her face. She motioned to the little dog jigging beside the door, its tail wagging as it looked up at them. "Here you go." She swung open the Dutch door and stepped inside.

Martin joined her, feeling his stomach growl.

Emily bent and lifted the dog. "What do you think?" She extended the furry ball toward Martin.

"What is he?"

"She's a cairn terrier." Without waiting for him to accept her invitation, she pressed the dog against his chest.

He drew back before grasping the squirming fluff ball into his arms but not before her pink tongue swiped his hand. He couldn't stop the flicker of a smile. The dog wiggled until her chin rested on his chest, and she looked into his face. Martin gazed back, his heart giving a little kick.

"She's quiet and well-behaved. I think she'd be perfect for you."

What would be perfect for him? What did she know about him but hearsay?

"Nessie's been spayed and is up to date on all her shots." Emily ran her hand along the dog's fur. "She's five, by the way. A healthy cairn terrier can live to be fourteen or fifteen."

"Nessie?" He tilted his head. "That's her name?"

The dog's ear's perked, and she tried to climb higher up his jacket.

Martin adjusted his grip but not before she licked his hand again.

"Cairns originated in Scotland. You know, the Loch Ness. That's how she got her name." Emily touched his arm. "And she's purebred, too. We have the papers."

Apparently she'd heard of his preference for purebreds. But that had changed, too. His attention shifted from his thoughts about the terrier to Emily's warm palm against his arm.

She held it there a moment before shifting her hand

and taking the dog from his arms. "Would you like to look at a different small dog? We have a beagle."

"No. They howl." He gazed again at the terrier. If Emily were accurate, and clearly she knew dogs, she had made a good choice for him. Quiet and well-behaved. That he could handle. He pulled his gaze from Emily's lovely eyes and turned his attention to the dog. "What do you think, Nessie? Want to come home with me?"

Emily's jaw dropped. "You want her?"

His single nod sent her rushing toward the office as if she feared he would change his mind. He stood at the desk while she became all business again. As she explained the paperwork, Martin sensed Emily was seeing him as more than just Nick's difficult brother.

When finished, she handed him the documents. "Now if you have any questions, Mr. Davis, just ask."

He folded the paperwork and jammed it into his pocket.

"Here you go." She snapped a leash onto the terrier's collar, and Martin grasped it, waiting for the dog to tug and run. Instead she stood there, her tail wagging. But when he headed for the door, the dog's personality changed. Martin gripped the leash as Nessie jerked him outside. For a small dog, she had power to spare. He tugged her back not knowing what else to do. She might be trained, but he wasn't.

Emily grinned, watching Martin charge out the door with Nessie. She'd been honest. The dog was quiet and well-behaved in her pen, but when she found freedom, she became difficult to handle. She'd neglected to tell him about the elderly woman who'd owned the dog and kept her inside most of the time. Getting out into the world was a new experience, and Nessie wanted to live and make the most of it.

So did Emily, but it hadn't happened and probably never would. It was just the way her life always seemed to be.

Martin's parked car caught her attention. Through the window, she watched him try to move Nessie off the driver's seat so he could get inside. He finally managed it.

When she'd first seen him in the office, she had been guarded in their conversation. Martin's reputation preceded him, and she'd felt intimidated. Yet she did her best to stand up for herself, rather than let the world run over her as she usually did.

The check he'd written caught her eye. Martin Davis. She studied his signature and drew in a deep breath. He had a flourish that whipped off into a curved line. Steph and Molly talked about him often, especially when she first started working at Time for Paws. Stories of Martin seemed a form of entertainment. When she'd seen him at the wedding, wow, she'd caught her breath. He was totally handsome, so unlike the vision she'd conjured in her mind.

What was it about him? She liked his eyes. They were rich brown like the saddles she'd seen in Western movies. Brown with flecks of gold, and though she knew eyes reflected attitude, Martin's hadn't. Walking behind him along the dog pens, she had admired his frame, six feet, she guessed, and lean with broad shoulders that added to his good looks. But Martin had the tendency of lowering his eyes, and that look gave him away. He might have a sharp tongue, but inside, she suspected he was as insecure and vulnerable as she was. She'd spent her life hiding her past, but Martin confounded her. He had so much going for him. What did he have to hide?

Tonight Martin had shown a softer side despite a few barbed comments. When he held Nessie, he'd melted like a cheap candle. And she'd caught him in a brief smile. His chin had dimpled below his even white teeth. She liked that, but it had made her selfconscious and she'd dragged her tongue over her teeth, fearing the sandwich she'd grabbed for dinner had left a telltale residue. She'd never liked her teeth. One was a little crooked so she tried to cover it when she smiled.

She glanced through the window again, her curiosity growing. Martin's car was still there, and she wondered if she should go out to see if he needed help. Instead, she gripped the desk and talked herself out of it. If she softened too much, she could be in trouble. He was single, she knew, and the kind of man that could make her life wonderful. She'd watched Molly and Steph marry, and though she had always figured marriage wasn't for her, her singleness seemed empty and lonely.

Wanting to get that nonsense out of her head, she focused on the check. He'd paid for Nessie's shots and added a generous donation for the dog shelter. Somewhere inside Martin Davis beat a kind heart. Someone just needed to find it. But definitely not her.

Emily edged forward and blocked the headlights' glare on the glass to see outside. Martin sat inside the car with Nessie sitting on his lap. The sight made her laugh. As she did, she turned away from the window before he spotted her.

The door to the pens remained ajar, but the noise inside had quieted. She strode to the door and slipped it closed before the dogs got riled again. The bell tinkled behind her, and she spun around. Martin stood inside with his hand on the doorknob. She caught her breath.

If he smiled now with those white teeth and that dimple, she couldn't cope.

Maintaining a semblance of control, Emily moved closer. "Is something wrong?"

As the last word left her mouth, a horn blasted outside.

Martin spun around and peered through the window. "You didn't tell me the whole story about that dog."

"Whole story?" She hoped her voice sounded steady.

"For one, she prefers the driver's seat or my lap."

"She's lonely."

Something flickered on his face, then faded. "I guessed that." He ran his hand over his jaw.

The horn blew again.

He waved his hand toward the window. "Any idea how to stop her from pawing at the horn?"

Emily chuckled. "Did you tell her to sit?"

Martin raised his shoulders, then lowered them. "About fifteen times." He opened the door and beckoned to her. "Look."

Feeling sorry for him just a wee bit, Emily strode to his side and looked at the car. Nessie stood on the steering wheel, gazing at him through the front windshield. When Martin didn't respond, the dog jumped from the steering wheel to the passenger window, her sharp barks penetrating the glass. Martin spun around and faced Emily. "I've been out there for five minutes, frustrated."

"It's the newness. She'll adjust. It takes time."

"Time? I just need a few tips on handling her."

"Nessie's had basic obedience training."

"Here's the situation. I don't have a clue how to…"

Emily pressed her lips together not to laugh. Mr.

Tough Guy had been weakened by a little fluffy dog. "Let me give you a brochure. We have dog obedience classes here a couple nights a week." She stepped to the desk, pulled out a pamphlet and handed it to him.

He grasped it without interest. "I thought the dog had basic training."

"But you haven't. The classes are for you."

"For me?" He glanced over his shoulder. "It's too quiet out there." He held up one finger and jerked open the door and headed outside.

In a moment, he was back, a look of relief on his face. "I peaked through the window. She's curled up on the backseat. I think she's asleep."

"I told you."

"This time." He eyed the brochure for a moment. "Okay, I suppose I need to understand the basics. Do you teach these classes?"

"Molly handles that, and sometimes Steph helps. I mainly run the office and take care of the dogs when I'm needed, and I own a dog-sitting and walking business." She hadn't meant to tell him that, but it was too late now. The problems Nick had experienced with his brother skittered across her mind. Martin leaned on everyone but himself. He needed to learn to take care of his own animals. Too late. His face had brightened, and Emily knew she was in trouble.

He rested his hand on the desk. "I—I might like to use your dog-walking service if you could fit me in. Some days I work long hours, and I hate to leave an animal alone for that long."

Emily gazed at his hand, noticing his long fingers with neatly trimmed fingernails. "I'm filled up right now." That was the best she could come up with quickly, and there was truth to her response, though she always tried to squeeze in every new costumer…except this time.

The brightness dimmed on Martin's face. "I'd still like your card if you have one. You never know."

She knew. She could handle dogs, but she couldn't handle Martin Davis. Even his hands intrigued her.

She dug in her pocket, pulled out a business card and handed it to him.

"Thanks." He eyed the card, then tapped the edge of it against his thumb. "Will you call me if you get an opening?"

Emily swallowed and forced herself to be firm. "I doubt that will happen. My customers stay with me a long time. They rarely drop the service." When she looked at his expression, she wished she'd been more gentle. But she had to stay in control.

Martin slipped the card into his pocket.

"You can call Molly about the training." She tilted her head toward his pocket. "The shelter's number is on there too."

He didn't look back. He grasped the knob and marched outside. Apparently Martin wasn't a man to accept the word No.

Martin bounded toward his car, trying to figure out what had gone wrong. *I doubt it.* Short but not sweet. Direct. No ifs, ands or buts. Though he'd always been able to manipulate people to do what he asked, he'd failed with dogs and obviously women. He'd never go to Molly or Steph for training. He'd feel uneasy. Feel stupid was more like it. He excelled in things. Martin Davis didn't fail. But he had. He'd thought he could intimidate Emily a little, but apparently he'd been wrong about that, too.

He stood outside a moment drinking in the fresh air as Emily's image filled his mind. When he'd first seen her, he'd taken a full sweep of her slender frame. She was tall like a reed. Thin and straight. She wore a long skirt that hung nearly to her ankles with that pale gray shirt that looked too big, as if she were drowning in her clothes. Beneath all that loose clothing he imagined a pretty woman with a nice figure who didn't want people to notice. She aroused his curiosity—his interest—and that scared him.

A question sizzled in his head. Women never attracted him, so why did this one? Perhaps he felt safer with her. She was younger than his forty-three years. Barely in her thirties, he guessed. He was too old for her even if he were interested, and he wasn't. He grabbed the door handle and pulled it open as he glanced into the backseat.

His pulse soared. "Nessie, no."

The terrier sprawled on the rear seat, gnawing on the handle of his attaché case. "What are you doing?"

She looked at him with innocent eyes. So had Emily.

Martin slammed his door and opened the back. Pushing Nessie aside, he jerked out his case, feeling the teeth marks embedded in the handle. "Bad dog." He shook his finger in her face.

She licked it.

He lowered his hand and wiped it on his pant leg. "Nessie, I wanted a quiet, little companion. Don't do this to me."

Martin tossed the attaché case on the floor, lifted Nessie in his arms, dodging her tongue, and placed her on the passenger seat. "We're going home. Be a good dog."

The terrier wagged her tail, and Martin took that as a yes.

If only he could have Emily eating out of his hand, but she'd nipped at it instead. She'd given him little hope. No hope. He started the car and backed away from the building. No hope? That was unacceptable.

# Chapter Two

Martin leaned over his dining room table, staring with blank eyes at the paperwork he had brought home. He usually never lugged work home. He stayed in his office to provide a good example to his employees. They needed to understand what devotion to a job meant. But he couldn't concentrate there. All day his mind flew back and forth to Nessie at home alone, fearing what she might do to his house. He had given up and come home at noon.

If Emily ran her own dog-walking business, she should have been able to squeeze Nessie in sometime during the day. She had encouraged him to adopt the dog but didn't want to help out otherwise.

Her face filled his mind, that impish look that was more a mask. At least when he smiled or frowned, that's how he felt and everyone knew it. He'd heard his sister-in-law say dogs were honest. If they liked a person they wagged their tails. If not, they let him know with a bark or a nip. Emily had an innocent, vulnerable look, but underneath, she had a sink-in-the-teeth bite. He should have guessed from that determined handshake.

Martin glanced into the living room and spotted Nessie curled beside the low front windows where the sun spread along the carpet. Emily had been right about one thing. Inside the house, Nessie seemed to behave.

He pictured Emily's slender hands, the way she kept her arms close to her sides with a slight swing, almost protective. He leaned back and closed his eyes, trying to relax and hoping to get her off his mind. The documents he'd brought home needed action on Monday. Since tomorrow was Saturday, he had the weekend to delve into them and be home with the dog. Hopefully Monday would start a better week.

Nessie gave a yip, and Martin opened his eyes. Her tail wagging and her ears perked in attention, she rose and headed toward him. He looked over his shoulder, hearing the sound.

When Nick strode into the room, Nessie skittered to him and sniffed his shoes. "I heard you had a new friend."

"Rumors travel fast." Martin rose to greet him.

"No rumor. This looks like a real live dog to me." He swooped the ball of fur into his arms while Nessie swiped his hand with kisses. "You cute little thing." He glanced at the terrier's belly. "Female, I see. You seem to have a dangerous bent toward women."

"It's a dog, Nick."

His brother chuckled. "You're asking for trouble when you bring a female into the house. You don't get along with them, remember?" He set Nessie on the floor.

Emily's face flashed through his mind, then Steph's. "You can't forget anything, can you?"

Nick strode closer and gave his shoulder a hug. "Just pulling your chain, bro."

"Fine, but enough's enough." He turned away and

strode to his recliner with Nessie following him with a longing look as if she wanted someone to play with her. One day he wanted to know about the dog's last owner. As he sank into the chair, he motioned toward the sofa. "How's Steph?"

"Better today. She did fine at work." He strode to the French-pane picture window and looked outside. Nessie pattered beside him and curled up into a ball in a sunny spot.

Martin's brow furrowed. "I thought her doctor told her to take it easy."

"She has been." Nick faced him. "Steph hired a young woman to come in and help with the dogs so she can do desk work and stay near the phone."

He acquiesced, hoping they were making the right decision. Nick oozed a positive attitude. Martin wished he could follow his brother's example. "Tell me about this woman that works at Time for Paws?"

"I don't know her. Steph just hired her a few—"

"Not the new one. I meant Emily."

Nick did a double take. "Emily? I don't know much about her." He gave Martin a scrutinizing look. "Why?"

Martin managed to act indifferent. "No reason. She has quite an attitude."

Nick sputtered into a guffaw. "Attitude? You're the king of attitude."

Struggling with a rebuttal, Martin covered his lack of words with a groan. "I'm working on it."

His brother stopped chuckling. "You are. I'll be the first to admit that." He crossed the room and plopped onto the sofa. "What happened yesterday?"

"Nessie gnawed the handle of my attaché case. This

morning I found my Italian belt covered with teeth marks."

Nick shrugged. "I can't help you with that. Anyway, I meant what happened between you and Emily?"

The past evening fell into Martin's mind, and he relayed her abrupt refusal to add him to her waiting list of customers. "I think she's heard too many rumors from Steph, and—"

Nick leaned forward. "Wait a minute. Steph doesn't spread rumors. If she said something it was true. You were horrible to her when you first met, and you know that, but you've made great strides, and I'm sure Steph has also mentioned that." He flung his hands in the air. "I don't know why they're talking about you now, anyway, but don't blame Steph."

Too late to undo his blunder. "I wasn't blaming Steph. I deserved every remark she might have made about me, but you know I'm working on my attitude. I monitored my comments with Emily." He revisited his evening with her. "Well, most of them."

Nick crossed his ankle over his knee and pulled up the sock. "You're upset because she wouldn't add you to her waiting list for what?"

"For her dog-walker services. You know that I work late sometimes, and—"

"And you don't have me to run your errands for you anymore."

Martin drew back at Nick's harsh comment. His stomach tightened. "Okay, I deserve that. But I haven't asked in a long time. You have your hands full with a new marriage and Steph's high-risk pregnancy. I worry about her, too."

"I know you do, and I appreciate it. That's the new side of you I really respect. You're thinking of others more than ever. Although I will admit, you were always good with Mom. Much better than I ever was."

"You're too tender-hearted."

Nick shook his head. "I suppose." He leaned back again, looking more at ease. "How are you getting along with Nessie?"

The terrier heard her name and made her way back to Nick. When she realized he wasn't going to pay attention to her again, she curled up at his feet and used his shoe as a pillow.

"She's a nice dog, but…" That but again. Martin wished he could remove the word from his vocabulary. "That's another thing about Emily. She suggested dog training, then pushed me off on Molly. I hate the idea of dog training, but if I decided to try it, I can't go to Molly. Her husband and I do business together. What happens if I do something that riles Molly? There goes that relationship."

Nick looked thoughtful. "And Steph isn't training now."

"Right." He didn't want to work with Steph, either. They had finally become friends. One wrong move could destroy that.

"Emily's been employed there less than a year. Maybe she doesn't train dogs."

"She must know something to be a dog-walker and sitter. She told me herself she has a lot of clients. I don't need classes. Just a few tips."

Nick looked toward the ceiling as if he'd find the answer there. He finally turned to Martin. "I can ask Steph if she'd talk with Molly. I don't know if it will do any good if Emily refuses, but Molly loves dogs, and I'm sure she wants you to do a good job with Nessie."

"That's all I want. I suppose I could look in the yellow pages for a trainer, but—"

"Hang on before you do that." He reached down and petted Nessie's head. "The poor dog has been shifted from one person to another. Time For Paws is familiar to her." He eyed Martin. "Should I talk with Molly?"

"Yes. Thanks. It's not really training for the dog. It's for me."

"You?" A silly grin stole to Nick's face and he chuckled. "Even better. Let me see what I can do."

Martin opened his mouth, then closed it. Let Nick laugh. One day the laugh would be on him. Nick had provided renewed motivation for Martin to be on his best behavior.

His pulse gave a kick. Talk about motivation, he sensed an ulterior motive going on in his brain, but he didn't want to face it. The least likely person in the world to interest him would be someone like Emily. Nothing in common but a dog. He pictured Emily's amazing eyes, her protective cover and her vulnerability. Then again, maybe they weren't so different.

Emily tightened the boxer's leash. Like most larger dogs, he had the strength of a bull, and she was glad she'd gained a little more muscle mass. She remembered taking her first couple of dog-walking jobs and feeling like the word "failure" was emblazoned on her forehead. When she'd let herself go a few years earlier, she looked gaunt, emaciated to some people, but now that her life had gotten back on track, she continued to work toward a healthier body. Dog-walking provided her a solid means to keep in shape.

Though she felt better about herself, she didn't want to hear comments about her nice figure or her looks.

People called her cute. She didn't see that either. Her biggest concern was working harder toward a healthier attitude. She wanted to forgot those horrible years that had stifled her for so long. Over and over she'd reminded herself that God had wiped the slate clean, but a slate filled with sin remained vivid in her mind.

She tightened the boxer's leash again while she located the key for his owner's house. When she walked inside, the dog darted for his dish, the leash trailing behind him. Emily filled his water dish, unhooked the leash, then located the dry dog food. She emptied some into the dog's bowl and watched him gobble it.

For a huge dog, this one had manners and always seemed happy when she arrived to walk him. Numerous times she'd been bullied by dogs she'd agreed to walk. She shook her head recalling some of the harrowing experiences, but with this boxer, she only had to battle his kisses.

Kisses. Martin Davis's lips filled her mind, and Emily's spine constricted. She hadn't seen the man since Thursday—four days ago. She shook her head to remove the image of his engaging lips and his beguiling eyes.

Emily stood a moment, gathering her wits, then hung the dog's leash on its hook and gave the boxer a final pet. As she headed for the door, the sound of her cell phone stopped her. She dug it from her purse and eyed the information. Molly. Molly didn't phone her often. Emily pushed the button, concerned something might be wrong. Maybe something with Steph. When she heard Molly's voice, she suspected she was right.

"You didn't tell me the whole story about Martin Davis."

Emily flinched. She'd thought she handled everything well. Fairly well. Martin's request for her card rang in her mind. Maybe she hadn't been kind when she said no, but she had to protect herself. "What do you mean? He didn't bring Nessie back, did he?" She hated to think of him doing that to get even, but that evening, he'd charged out the door as if he'd spotted a tiger.

"No. No threats, but we have to keep our clients happy. Steph said he was nice enough when he talked with Nick, but he was upset that Nessie chewed the handle on his attaché case. You didn't tell me that."

"I didn't know." She shifted the boxer away from the door and opened it. "She must have done it when he came back into the office to ask some questions." She decided to avoid the details. Emily slipped outside and checked the lock before heading for her car.

Molly gave a soft chuckle. "Well, that's not all. The other morning Nick dropped in at Martin's and heard Nessie had gnawed his Italian leather belt during the night." Molly's exhale sounded over the line. "I don't suppose you warned him."

"You should have seen him, Molly. He even smiled when Nessie licked his hand." She stood beside her car, shifting to keep the sun from her eyes. "She'd been good with us, and I didn't think of it."

"She had toys here, not expensive leather belts and briefcases."

Fear of what Molly might want her to do crept through her mind. She hoped she was wrong. "What does he want? Us to replace his belt?"

The line was silent a moment. "No. He wants training, and he would rather not take classes from me, because of his relationship with Brent. That's what Nick said. They do business together, and...I don't know, but he told Nick he'd be uncomfortable. So it's your job. He doesn't know you."

And Emily wanted to keep it that way.

"He's willing to pay extra for private home lessons."

"Private? Why?" She'd be expected to spend time alone with him. She couldn't keep him out of her thoughts now, and she'd only seen him once. Twice. The wedding flashed in her mind.

"You know men…especially this one. They have pride. He's probably embarrassed that the dog knows more than he does."

Emily stifled a chuckle, thinking of Martin's know-it-all attitude. Then reality struck. "I'd rather not, Molly." In the background, a dog's bark echoed through the phone line.

"Are you afraid of him, or his reputation?"

"Probably his reputation. He was a little snarky Thursday." Her mind tripped back to that day.

"Maybe he was trying to be funny and failed. You need to understand his bark is worse than his bite, and he doesn't bark as much as he did."

That gave Emily a rallying vote of confidence. "I'm still not convinced." But she had changed. She had the Lord to thank for that. She'd witnessed Martin had changed, too. His tenderness with Nessie filled her mind and his occasional grin.

"I can't force you, but it would be a favor to me, and Steph, too. Martin's her brother-in-law."

Emily let the thought rattle around in her mind. She wanted to protect herself but from what? A man. He wouldn't give her a second look so what was she worried about?

A sigh escaped her. "I'll see what I can do." She tucked the cell phone between her ear and shoulder as she pulled a hunk of paper and a pen from her purse.

"Give me the address and phone number." Resting the paper against her car, she scribbled down the information. "Got it."

"Thanks. I realize this is beyond the call of duty."

She could picture Molly's grin. "I know."

She closed her phone and slipped it back into her handbag. Something about Martin irked her but intrigued her at the same time. He had gall, expecting a personal home visit. Dog shelters didn't provide individual service. They did the best they could to save dogs' lives by making them adoptable. But Martin had clout, and from all she'd heard, he liked getting his own way...unless that had changed, too.

A revelation came to her while talking with Molly, and Emily wanted to take care of that first before calling Martin. And she needed to get her mind in order. She wanted the tone of their meeting to be professional.

Once on the road, Emily realized Martin's house would be easy to find. He lived next to Steph's old home, from before she married Nick. Thinking of Steph, her mind clicked back to her first days at the dog shelter. Steph ran her doggie day care in the back of the building while Molly owned the shelter in the front. Both women loved dogs as much as she did, and it seemed like providence when Emily stumbled on the job shortly after the shelter had opened.

Dogs and three women who loved them. Meeting Steph and Molly had been a blessing.

Emily slowed as she approached the next corner. She veered into the right lane and turned. Glad she had the idea, she headed for a pet supply store certain that Martin hadn't planned ahead. Dogs needed toys, things they could chew, and she wanted to pick up a training device to help Martin. He'd said he knew nothing about working with dogs so a quick lesson seemed suitable.

Shopping took only a minute, and Emily was back in the car. She stared at her handbag. She had to make the call. Thinking of tropical breezes and a lovely sunset, she calmed her thoughts. The technique worked for her. A Caribbean vacation had always been her dream. So romantic. The word jarred her. She forced her mind to a quiet place, then dug into her handbag and pulled out her cell phone.

After locating the scrap of paper with Martin's phone number, she faced the keypad. Her fingers hesitated as she pressed the numbers. "Get a grip." The phone rang and in minutes, Martin's voice rolled through the line.

"This is Emily Ireland. Molly asked me to stop by so we could talk. Is today okay?"

"Perfect." Relief sounded in his voice. "Do you know where I live?"

She said she did and hung up as soon as she could. After tossing her phone back into her bag, she turned the key in the ignition, pulled into traffic and retraced the route. Before long, her car nosed into Martin's driveway. She'd never paid attention before, but today she sat a moment to drink in the homey look of his property.

Cedar-shake siding gave it a Cape Cod look, except for its sprawling size. Dormers accented the front windows, and a long porch enclosed by a railing added an old-fashioned look. Though the landscape offered low spreading evergreen shrubs beneath the dormer windows, Emily longed to see flowers. In spring, tulips and daffodils blossomed in beds around many homes. Grape hyacinths clustered in borders, but not here. Instead, a shade tree grew from a raised island with large stones and low-lying ground cover. If the house were hers, she would add flowers. Nothing seemed to make a home prettier than bright blossoms.

The vision made her ache for what might have been if she'd had a different life. She drew in a long breath, and instead of letting the mood affect her, she grasped the package and left the car. The closer she strode to the front door the more her nerves came out of hiding. He'd asked her to come. It wasn't as if she was making a surprise visit.

Emily stood for a moment to gather her confidence, then pushed the bell. She heard a pleasant chime from within and waited.

The door opened, and Martin gaped at her a moment before he spoke. "That was fast." He pushed open the screen door. "I didn't know you were so close."

She took a step backward. "If it's a problem, I can—"

"It's not a problem." A faint grin slipped to his mouth. "Come in."

Emily stepped inside, her gaze lowering to Martin's stockinged feet against the stone-tiled foyer. Her stomach tightened. The image of Martin Davis looking as homey as his house seemed unreal. She'd never pictured him in jeans and a pair of socks looking like a regular homebody. He'd even flashed her a smile. The vision rushed through her.

Past the foyer, a family room lay in front of her where she could see patio doors leading outside. When he motioned her to come in further, she clamped her jaw to hold back her reaction. The foyer flowed into a huge living room with a stone fireplace and cathedral ceiling. Across the thick carpet she spotted a dining area. She loved the large open room, and when she looked at him, she couldn't help but tell him. "This is wonderful for entertaining."

"I wouldn't know."

She winced at his abrupt response. A distant sound distracted her followed by a scratching noise that caused her concern. "What's that noise? Nessie?"

"I locked her in the laundry room where she can do less damage."

Emily's back tightened. "No." She gave him a piercing gaze before she could stop herself.

He staggered back a step and looked at her with wide eyes. "What?"

"That's not the way to train a dog."

"No kidding."

His sarcastic tone didn't stop her. "Then why did you do it?"

His looked soften. "Emily, I don't know how to work with a dog. That's why I called Molly."

She looked away, startled that she'd gotten so mouthy. "Let Nessie out of the laundry room. Then we can talk."

He nodded and headed for the doorway off the dining room, his expression more like the man she'd seen when she walked into the house.

Although he hadn't invited her, Emily followed. When she stepped into the kitchen, she quelled an appreciative moan. Expansive cabinets were highlighted by a large island. On the far side, a breakfast nook sat beside broad windows that looked into the backyard. She could imagine eating there in the morning, watching the birds flap their wings in a birdbath and squirrels skittering in the trees. She'd dreamed of a comfortable home with a pretty yard.

The scratching noise stopped, and Nessie darted into

the room, her nails tapping against the wooden floor. She skidded to a stop beside her.

Emily lifted the terrier in her arms. Nessie's tongue lapped across her hands before swiping her cheek. She cuddled the terrier, feeling her heartbeat pounding against her palm. "You poor little thing." She nuzzled her face in the dog's fur.

When she lifted her head, Martin watched her, a troubled look etching his face. "I didn't think putting her in the laundry room was cruel."

"No, but she's frightened." Nessie's heartbeat slowed and she squirmed to get down. "Remember, she lost her owner, then spent two days with us, and now she's with you. Can you imagine how you'd feel being taken from your home and locked in a cell like a prisoner, and then when you were bailed out and thinking you were saved, you were locked up again?"

Martin ran his fingers through his hair. "I didn't think of it like that."

His contrite expression wrenched her heart. When he lowered his hand, she gazed at his dark hair now ruffled by his fingers. He wore it with no part, short and thick with a natural wave. She longed to bury her hand in its thickness.

As if he heard her, Martin smiled.

Smile? She didn't want him to smile. The pit of her stomach fell and rose, pressing air from her lungs. This yo-yo man vacillated from intolerable to lovable in the blink of an eye.

Her frustration weakened. "Can we talk?" She lowered Nessie to the floor.

He motioned behind her. "Let's sit in the family room." He pointed to the doorway.

As she moved ahead, he stopped in front of the refrigerator. "Iced tea?"

Emily thought of saying no, but nerves had dried her throat. "Yes, please. No sugar." Though eager to view the family room, she watched him pull out glasses and pour the drinks. He looked comfortable in the kitchen, his stockinged feet padding along the oak planks. Who would have thought that Martin had a homey side in him? But he did, and she liked it.

Martin tilted his head toward the family room. "You didn't need to wait."

"I like watching you work in the kitchen." The words sailed out with a mind of their own.

His grin brightened as he handed her the tea. "I find that interesting."

She shrugged, wishing she had a snappy response. "I don't have much of a kitchen. It's a studio apartment."

His grin faded, and she wished she hadn't admitted it. She took one last sweeping gaze of his spacious kitchen before moving into the family room. When she did, sunlight filtered through the glass door onto the carpet, leaving sunny splotches and changing its color from beige to gold. Sunshine also radiated from above, and she lifted her gaze to the cathedral ceiling with a skylight. Ultimate luxury. She'd never known anything like this. She turned in a circle, searching to see if he'd thought to purchase a doggie bed for Nessie, a place she could call her own. She saw none.

Across from another fireplace—how many did one man need?—she eyed the wide patio door.

Martin stood in the doorway, watching her, but she didn't care. She'd never been in a house like this. None of her clients had a home of this size. Nessie pit-patted beside her as Emily ambled across the room and looked through the glass. The large yard spotted with shade trees and shrubs looked inviting but lacked the flowers she loved.

She glanced over her shoulder. "I know it's cool, but could we sit outside? Nessie probably needs to run, anyway."

"Why not?" He followed her as she unlocked the door and pushed it open.

Nessie shot through the doorway, sniffing the ground and heading for an area in the back of the property.

"How about there?" Martin motioned toward the chairs arranged around an umbrella table.

Emily strolled over, forcing her mind to focus on why she'd come. The house and the attractive man gave her a fairy-tale feeling. Though she loved those children's tales, she knew real life didn't always have happy endings.

When she sat, she still clutched the paper sack in her hand. She set the package on the table and sipped the tea. The condensation wetted her fingers, and she wiped them on her jeans, then placed the glass on a coaster and gazed toward Nessie across the yard. "You have no flowers." The thought shot from her mouth.

He looked up, peering at her as if she'd lost her mind. "What?"

Uneasy with her bluntness, she sank deeper into the chair cushion. "Your yard. It's beautiful, but…"

His eyes searched hers, and a prickling sensation ran down her arms.

"Maybe it's a woman's thing." He gazed across the lawn. "My mom always had flowers in the yard."

His mom. The impact of his statement was unexpected. She'd never had anyone in her life she wanted to call Mom. Sometimes the word mother even clung to her tongue. Her hand trembled as she looked at Martin and thought of his home. She shouldn't be sitting here like a friend. This wasn't her world, and if she loved it too much, she—

"Is that for Nessie?"

His voice tugged her from her thoughts. When she looked up, his finger aimed at the sack. She lowered her hands to her lap, willing them to steady and begging her heart to stop pounding. "It's for both of you, really." Her voice sounded breathy. She sucked in air. "You can open it."

Martin unwound the top of the bag and looked inside, emptying out a raw hide, a squeaky toy, and tug rope. He squeezed the plastic hotdog, releasing its high-pitched squeal. "Thank you so much." He grinned. "I didn't buy a thing for her." He raised on one hip and slipped his hand into his back pocket, pulling out his wallet, his face so tender her knees weakened.

Panic filled her as Emily shook her head. "No. It's a gift." Her heart pummeled her chest as she rose. "Nessie needs a spot to call her own, too. Everyone needs a place..." She dragged in some air. "A place to call home." She stepped back from the table, overwhelmed by her feelings of sadness and fear.

Martin frowned and leaned forward, his wallet still clutched in his hand. "What are you doing?"

She backed away. "I have to leave. I'm sorry."

"But what about—"

"I'm sorry." She rushed to the patio door. "Thank you for the tea." She dashed through the house and onto the porch, as if midnight had struck and she had to make her getaway.

# Chapter Three

Martin stood in the floral shop eyeing the bouquets, but his mind remained on Emily. Since she walked out three days earlier, he'd been baffled about what he'd done. They were talking and she was fine until she jumped up and ran off. Racking his brain, he couldn't think of what he'd done that might have offended her. He'd been stirred by her thoughtful gift. She didn't have money for dog toys. Anyone who lived in a studio apartment likely couldn't afford much. He'd only tried to pay her for her thoughtfulness.

He could hear the toy hotdog squeal in his head. Nessie loved it, and Martin admired Emily's kindness.

The toys for Nessie triggered another thought. When he had gone to throw the bag in the trash, he felt something else inside, a small clicker of some kind. It certainly didn't look like a toy. Glad he found it, Martin had tucked it away. He needed to call Emily about it. He closed his eyes, giving his idea a second thought. Having no clue what happened that day, Martin didn't want to get his head chewed...like a rawhide. Maybe asking Steph about it was a better idea.

The scent of flowers drew his mind back to the floral display. He focused on the bouquets. Roses? Carnations? He wanted something cheerful for his mother. When he spotted the mixed bouquet of spring flowers, he decided that was it. Bright, cheery and full of hope. Spring always left him with expectations—rebirth of nature and hopefully his own rebirth as he worked to alter his attitude and his life. Hopeful, yes, but sometimes that job seemed hopeless. Emily's race from the yard had sparked that thought.

With the bouquet wrapped and paid for, Martin slipped into his car and headed for Waltonwoods to visit his mother. Although she'd resisted moving to an assisted living residence after her stroke, she'd given in and now was adjusting well to residing in the independent living facility. Martin's guilt had subsided. He turned onto Walton Boulevard and pulled into the visitor parking. Grabbing the bouquet, he headed inside, signed in and took the elevator to his mother's apartment. A small placard next to the door read Julia Davis. The Julia was printed in a large font. Identity. Everyone needed it, especially those who'd lived a full life and sometimes struggled to find a purpose.

When his mother opened the door, her eyes twinkled as he remembered from childhood—except those times he'd done something wrong, when he had seen hurt in her eyes. Martin kissed his mother's cheek and placed the bouquet in her arms. His chest tightened seeing pleasure on her face.

She buried her nose in the blossoms. "They're lovely, Martin. And they smell so sweet." She cradled the bouquet as if it were a baby and motioned him inside.

The sting of fleeting years pricked Martin's senses as he strode across the room and sank onto the sofa.

He didn't envision the joy of holding his own offspring. He'd remained single since his divorce, ashamed that he'd been abandoned by his wife. Her reason had left him staggering: he wasn't a good husband. That's what she'd said. He'd spent his days working to make a home and hopefully to provide well for a family, but Denise had walked out without giving him a chance and with no desire to make it work.

He'd married for better or worse, never expecting he would be the worse for Denise. Nick encouraged him to get over it, but Nick hadn't fared much better with his first fiancé walking away before the wedding. But Nick had found love again, lessening Martin's bitterness. Nick and Steph made a great couple, and now there was a baby on the way. The knife twisted deeper.

"Is something wrong?"

Martin jerked his head upward, sorry he'd let his mind wander. "Not a thing. In fact, I have some good news."

Her face brightened. "Really? Is it someone new in your life?"

Martin squirmed as a vision of Emily filled his mind. "She's a cairn terrier named Nessie. A bundle of fur." He rose to evade the disappointment on her face and grasped the flowers. "Do you have a vase for these, Mom?" Rather than looking at her, he scanned her small apartment for a container, the kitchen taking a corner of her living room with a bedroom and bath beyond.

"Martin."

He glanced her way.

"Look on top of the cabinet there." She pointed. "Use that crystal one. Your father brought that home for me once filled with roses."

He reached above the cabinet and lowered the vase, recalling how often he'd seen it filled with flowers in their home when he was a teen. Flowers. The memory of Emily in his yard slipped through his mind until he refocused. "Dad was a good man." He found the courage to face her.

A sweet smile curved her mouth. "I didn't know if you boys realized that. He was strict and not always there for you when you needed him."

A void rushed through him and he remembered his yearnings to have his father notice him the way he noticed Nick, but he provided for them and cared in his own way. "We knew."

He turned his attention to filling the vase with water and jamming the flowers into it. He had no idea how to arrange them. "What do you think?" He stepped past the cabinets and held the vase so she could see it.

"I think you should let me meet your new pet."

Though she'd faltered over her words, Martin realized how much she'd improved since her stroke, but he also caught her message. His stomach knotted. She wanted to be with him or Nick and not here. But they both had jobs and... "We'll work something out now that you're walking better."

"I've tried." She turned her attention to the flowers, sending him a crooked smile left from her stroke. "Do you need help with those?"

"Probably."

She beckoned him to bring her the flowers.

"Sorry. I don't do arranging." Martin chuckled as he approached her, but he didn't feel the humor. He shifted a wooden TV tray closer to her chair and set the flowers on it. "What do you need?"

"Scissors." She motioned toward the corner of her cabinets. "In the end drawer there."

He opened it and found the scissors.

"And some paper towel."

Nick unrolled the toweling and brought it to her with the scissors, then sat in the nearest chair to watch. Her earlier comment about bringing her home for a visit had unsettled him. He and Nick should be more available to her, but somehow life got in the way. He visited regularly, but his mother wanted more. He lowered his head, knowing that visiting this way meant he could leave after an hour or so when it was convenient and then get on with life.

But this was her life in this limited space with only a few mementos of the past, like the vase that meant so much to her. He closed his eyes a moment, wishing life didn't hurt so much. But the Lord promised believers Heaven, where pain and sadness would be gone. He forced his head upward and watched his mother manipulate the flowers, clipping off an end here and sliding in a stalk of greenery there until the flowers looked like a real arrangement.

"Good job, Mom."

She grinned, adding the final few flowers, her veined hands, fragile and almost transparent, working deftly with the blossoms.

"Arranging flowers is sort of a lesson in life, Martin. Sometimes you have to clip away a bad stem or shorten a blossom so it doesn't overpower a more delicate one. You have to discard ones that are broken or dead to make room for the flowers that are still lovely."

Discard the dead and broken. Why couldn't he do that? Dead dreams and broken promises. Cut them away so they didn't overpower what was worthy and beautiful.

"When you tuck something beautiful beside the plain,

each enhances the other." She turned the vase around to face him. "What do you think?"

"It looks great. Just like a professional."

She waved his words away, and he grinned seeing both hands functioning now after the stroke that had left her with so many problems.

He rose. "Where do you want the vase?"

"On the table there." She pointed to the small dining table. Her eyes drifted from the arrangement to him. "Tell me about the dog."

"I adopted her from Time for Paws, where Steph works."

Her eyebrows raised. "From the shelter?"

Her tone let him know she hardly believed he'd obtained a dog from there. "Yes. She's five, but her life expectancy is three times that."

She gave him a motherly look and pushed the table to the side. "I suppose Steph helped you select this dog."

He fought his growing anxiety. "No. I decided to stop on my way home from work and take a look. The part-time girl was there."

"You mean Emily?" Hearing her name caused his pulse to skip. "I met her at the wedding. Very sweet."

"I suppose." His heel tapped against the floor, and he pressed his hand against his knee to control it.

His mother noticed, and he squirmed while she studied him. "Emily's nice, don't you think?"

He drew back and gave up on quieting his knee. He knew what his mother was getting at. If she were still living in her home, he would be invited to dinner once a week to meet some young woman who was the daughter of a friend or a friend of a friend. She believed God meant everyone to be in twos. Just like the ark. Hear that, Noah?

Martin gave up. When his mother probed for information, she knew how to do it. He'd run into the same technique as a child. He couldn't get away with anything, but then, he rarely wanted to. As the oldest child with his parents' full attention, he'd demanded much of himself, not wanting to disappoint them.

Emily became the topic of conversation for the next few minutes. He told her about his problem with Nessie, and how Emily had dropped by with the toys.

"That's strange. Why would she do that?"

"I'd asked her about obedience training, and..." His cell phone vibrated in his pocket.

"Yes, I'm sure Emily would be happy to help."

Knowing his mother, she'd never stop. Never did when he was a boy, and she wouldn't now. Instead of trying to respond, he dug out the phone and flipped it open. His chest constricted. Emily. He stared at her number, then closed the lid.

"Important?"

No. His stomach rolled. Yes, it was important. He wanted to know why Emily had called. "It's nothing."

"Are you sure?"

He looked away. "I'm sure." Then he rose. "Mom, what's on your mind? Do you think every time my phone rings it's some woman you can trap into falling in love with me? It's not going to happen."

"Martin. No one needs to be trapped. You're a handsome man with a successful business, a lovely home, and a new dog." She shook her head. "And I want you to have the joy of being a father one day."

"A father?" He shook his head. "I need a wife first."

"Now, that's what I want to hear." She rubbed her hands together. "Let's work on that."

*Let's?* Martin leaned over and kissed his mother's cheek. "I have to go, Mom. I'll put that in your capable hands."

She grinned as he turned away. He'd never get that idea out of her head.

Emily leaned against the shelter's storage room doorway and clutched her cell phone. Calling had been a bad idea. Martin hadn't answered, and though he might have a good reason, she suspected he didn't want to talk to her. She'd pondered her behavior for the past three days trying to make sense out of it. When she'd sat in his lovely yard talking to him, she'd had an overwhelming feeling that she didn't belong there. That was it.

Yet somewhere deep inside her, Emily wanted to apologize. How could he ever understand her behavior unless he knew her, and he didn't. That's how she wanted it. But then, when he pulled out his wallet... It had been too much.

A sound caused her to turn as Molly appeared in the doorway, looking slim again after the birth of her new baby Zachariah. Such a big name for a little boy. Emily glanced at her watch. "Is it that time already?"

"Brent came home early so I left him on diaper and bottle duty."

"Good for you. Make him work." Emily managed a smile. She shifted a dog food bag against the wall and uncoiled her back, then pulled up her shoulders and sucked in her belly to force her spine to straighten.

Molly eyed her a second, then put her fists on her hips. "Are you okay?"

"I'm fine. Just tired. I haven't slept well for the past couple nights."

Molly's brows arched. "The past couple nights? Is

that my fault, Emily? Don't tell me you had a bad time with Martin. I shouldn't have insisted you—"

Martin's name shot through Emily like a dart. "No. He was fine."

"Really?"

She nodded and looked away before Molly asked anything more. "I picked up a few things on the way to his house—a rawhide and a couple of other toys... and a clicker." She'd forgotten it was in the bag until yesterday.

"I hope he paid you."

Her pulse skipped again. "No. It—it was a gift."

"A gift? Be careful. He could easily take advantage of your kindness. Martin can do that to people." She slipped her arm around Emily's shoulders and gave her a hug. "The Lord will put extra stars in your crown though. That was nice of you."

Stars in her crown. Emily doubted if she'd have a crown. Getting into Heaven would be blessing enough. "He seemed different Wednesday." In stockinged feet.

Molly squeezed her shoulder. "Steph gets along with him now."

Martin's image settled in her mind. He's been friendly enough. "But people can also slip back into old habits."

Molly nodded, but her expression had darkened, and it made Emily suspect she was thinking about Emily's past. Shortly after she'd started working at the shelter, Molly had spotted the scars on her wrists. Even her watch and bracelet didn't cover them completely. Molly had never asked for details, and she hoped it would stay that way. Emily pushed her thoughts aside and changed the subject. "We had a good day. Two new adoptions. Buster and Rosey are gone."

"Wonderful." She took a step toward the door before turning back. "How did the lesson go?"

"Lesson?" Her stomach twisted, fearing Molly would be upset if she knew Emily had walked out. "I gave him the toys and left." She focused on Molly. "What's wrong?"

"You."

"Me?" She kept her hand steady as she pressed her index finger against her chest.

A grin slipped to Molly's face. "You're blushing."

Emily pulled her hand from her chest and cupped her cheek in her palm. "I don't know what you're talking about. My face isn't hot."

Molly's grin broadened. "You blushed when you mentioned Martin." She faced her, her arms akimbo. "What's going on?"

"What could go on? I've known him a week, and that includes today." Her lips pressed together, but she forced them apart. "I don't know where you came up with that dumb idea." Yes, she found him attractive. Yes, he stirred some emotion, but...

"I fell in love with Brent a couple days after I met him." Molly uncoiled her arms. "Maybe not in love, but I fell in deep like."

"Deep like." Emily chuckled a little too heartily. "That's a new one."

Silence.

Molly gave her a playful smirk. "I don't think so. We'll just wait and see."

"You'll have to wait a long time."

Molly grinned and strode toward the office while Emily watched her go, feeling helpless. Yes, she'd thought about Martin and about Nessie. More about Nes... Maybe they'd both been on her mind, but she certainly hadn't fallen in love or even like. Actually, she'd been confused. Where did Molly come up with something so ridiculous? She turned away, opened the dog food bag and continued filling the dogs' dishes. Her day ended when Molly arrived, but she never left a job half finished.

The dogs wagged and wiggled to get to the food. They looked happy and healthier than some had looked when they'd arrived. Homeless dogs, abandoned dogs broke her heart. She and they were kindred spirits.

Emily grabbed her handbag and said goodbye to Molly as she hurried through the office and stepped outside. She didn't want to talk with Molly about falling into anything.

Outside, she stopped and drew in a deep breath. The spring air filled her lungs and refreshed her in the same way the Holy Spirit had filled her with hope. In the sunlight, she leaned against her car and thought. Martin had hung on her mind many times during the day. Did he give Nessie the rawhide? Would he remember to purchase a doggie bed?

She opened her car door, but instead of climbing in, she leaned against the sedan, thinking about the call she'd made to him. She pulled out her cell phone and checked for messages. Nothing. Maybe she should call again and—

No. She'd called once. If he wanted to talk with her, he'd call back. If he found the clicker in the bag, he may have figured out how to use it. He didn't need her.

Martin opened the door from the garage and heard Nessie's nails clicking across the kitchen. Before he closed the door, the dog had reached the laundry room, her tail wagging. He bent down and petted her. Her dark eyes with long wispy brows gazed at him as if he were a hero. His chest tightened. Some men had children look at them like that. At least he had the dog.

When he closed the door, Nessie skittered off the way she'd come, and when Martin stepped into the kitchen, he found her posed by her dish.

"Hungry?"

Her tail wagged as he headed for the bag of dog food. He added nuggets to her dish. And refreshed her water, then strolled into the family room and wandered to the patio door. In moments, Nessie padded to his side. He slid open the glass and let her out. She'd been pretty good since she had had the toys to gnaw. The clicker didn't make sense to him so it lay on the kitchen counter. He guessed that's why Emily had called.

An empty feeling settled in his chest. She would never come back. He sensed it. Success wasn't his friend when it came to relationships with people. His mother had always seen his good side, but others? He didn't want to go there.

He stepped onto the patio, pulled his cell from his pocket and settled into a chair at the umbrella table, the phone clutched in his hand. A cooler breeze drifted past, smelling like rain. Martin looked into the gloomy sky, noting the heavy clouds that had covered the sun. He hated dismal days. They made him feel worse.

The cell phone warmed his palm, and his chest tightened as he hit dial. It rang twice. He held his breath. As he mustered control, her hesitant voice met his ears.

"I couldn't answer earlier, Emily. Sorry."

"I—I didn't want to bother you, but—"

"You're no bother." He drew in a quick breath. "I'm glad you called." He fought his instinct to ask her why she'd run off. "You left something in the bag when you were here that I think belongs to you."

"The clicker. I bought that for you. It's a method to train Nessie. I—"

Silence ran through the line, and he opened his mouth but held back, knowing she had something else on her mind.

"I'm sorry about running off. I'd meant to show you how to use it."

"Emily, listen. Let's back up. You don't need to apologize. I know something happened, and I feel badly. Would you drop by so we can talk? Or if you prefer, I'll meet you somewhere."

More silence.

He couldn't bear it and drew in a lengthy breath to calm himself. "The toys worked like a charm. Nessie hasn't eaten a leather belt or the handle off of anything."

Her faint chuckle whispered through the line. "That's good."

His foot tapped against the patio tiles as he waited for her to respond to his suggestion about meeting. Waited for her to say anything. He forced himself to remain silent.

"There's a park not far from you," she said finally. "It's on—"

"I know where it is. I used to…Nick used to walk Suzette there."

"I can be there in a few minutes. I'm not too far away."

"Great." He loosened his grip on the phone. "I'll see you there."

"Bring Nessie."

He agreed and clicked off, his mind racing. She'd

apologized. He still didn't know why, but it was a beginning. He dashed inside, slipped out of his dress pants and tugged on his jeans and a polo shirt. Nessie was at the patio door when he returned to the family room, and he let her inside. As he headed for the laundry room for her leash, Martin grasped the clicker from the kitchen counter and slipped it into his pocket.

Nessie grew excited when she saw the leash. She needed to be walked, and he'd tried, but he hadn't learned how to master the dog and the tether.

"Come on, little girl. We're going for a walk." He maneuvered Nessie to the front door and strode outside with the dog barreling ahead.

The park was close, but Nessie added time to the walk by tangling his legs in the leash. He had no idea what to say to the dog to keep her heading forward at a stride, not a sprint. A car passed him as he neared the grassy area. It slowed and pulled up to the curb. Emily slipped out and waited for them, a sympathetic grin on her face. His heart began to skip.

"Nessie did a great job getting you here."

He shrugged and added a grin. "I told you I need practice."

Emily strode toward the grass, glancing over her shoulder as they followed. "Did you think to bring the clicker?" She wore a pair of slacks beneath a long shirt, the sleeves rolled up. The clothes looked as if she'd borrowed them from a brother.

Yet no matter what she wore, he found her attractive. In the sunlight, he noticed her creamy skin. She wore only a trace of makeup. He liked the natural look. It fit her. Honest and simple.

He'd wanted to talk with her first, but apparently she

wanted to work with the dog. He drew in a breath, dug into his pocket and pulled out the gadget.

She opened her palm, and he dropped it in. "We use this to enforce good behavior. When Nessie does something right, you click this and give her a treat. Eventually, you can either click or offer the treat, and she'll understand." Emily glanced at him as if she'd expected him to bring along the dog food nuggets.

He watched while Emily demonstrated, and then he tried using the gadget, but Martin noticed most of the time she was evading his eyes. He was captured by the innocence in her face, almost as if life was a bus she'd missed and she was waiting for another to pass by. That interested him. He winced, not wanting to admit it was more than interest. He was attracted to Emily.

When he didn't respond, she turned his way, her eyes questioning. "Is something wrong?"

"Are you avoiding me?"

She almost did a double take. "I'm here. Does that look like I'm avoiding you?"

Her response frustrated him. She'd redirected the question. "Avoidance can mean more than absence."

A faint scowl flickered across her face.

"Did I do something the other day when you darted off? If I did, I apologize. I thought we were—"

Her hand jutted upward, accidentally sounding the clicker, but she didn't grin. "It wasn't you. I had something on my mind, and I needed to leave."

"But so suddenly?"

This time she searched his face with an intense look as if wanting to continue, but the tightness of her lips warned him not to pursue it further.

She eyed her watch, turning a little as if she didn't want him to know what time it was. When she turned back, she knelt down and petted Nessie. "You have the idea, right?" She edged her gaze upward.

He sensed she'd become antsy. "Let me try again. This time walking with her. That's when I have most of my problems."

"I noticed."

The lilt of her voice had a playful ring, a total change from moments earlier. A drop of rain hit his cheek, and Martin glanced up, spotting a dark cloud overhead. Emily hadn't seemed to notice, and he didn't mention the rain. He strode away, holding the leash shorter and tighter, saying "good girl" with a click as Nessie stayed close. He sensed he was pressing his luck when she spotted a bird and tugged at the leash. He drew her back, and when she pattered beside him, he clicked again and reached down to pet her. Her tail whipped like a flag in the wind.

A raindrop hit his hand as another struck his nose. He turned back, maneuvering Nessie toward Emily. Before he took a step, the sky opened, and rain poured. He bent down and scooped Nessie into his arms, hightailing toward the street while Emily waved him forward as she slipped into her car.

He opened the passenger door and jumped inside, putting Nessie on his lap. "That came on fast." His shirt stuck to his back and Nessie's fur dripped rain onto his lap. When he focused on Emily, her hair lay plastered against her cheeks, making her look even more guileless and sweet than he could remember. "Thanks."

"You're soaked." She covered her grin with her fingertips.

"So are you." He grinned back.

She turned the key in the ignition, switched on the wipers, and pulled away. He tried to make small talk, but she seemed distracted. He suspected she didn't like to drive in a rainstorm. A zap of lightning split the sky followed by a distant roll of thunder that sounded above the slap of the windshield wipers.

Emily rolled into the driveway, and he eyed the water dripping from her hair. "You should come in for a minute and dry off."

"I'll be home shortly, but thanks."

Her playful tone had vanished again, and he decided not to push it. "When will we get together again?"

A frown shot to her face as she turned toward him.

"I mean for some more help with Nessie, and I'd still like you to walk—"

"I'm not the one to do this." She blinked at him, her frown deepening. "You should call Molly about the lessons. She has the experience. And Nessie's doing fine."

But I'm not. The words longed to be spoken, but they held too much meaning to him. "I thought—"

"Really, you have the idea. You're doing fine."

Her anxious look prodded him to nestle the dog in his arms and push open the door. "Thanks for the ride." He shook his head, his eyes searching hers. "I'm sorry if—"

"It's not you, Martin. I told you that."

She lowered her head, and he had nothing to do but step into the rain, close the door, and run for the house while Emily pulled away, leaving him confused and empty.

# Chapter Four

The wipers smacked against the windshield as Emily turned the corner. Though rain splattered the glass, her tears blurred her sight even more. She took a deep breath, releasing it in a whoosh of air. The vision of Martin's face stirred her guilt. Confusion creased his brow with a deep furrow and disappointment glazed his eyes. The man had done nothing to her except arouse memories.

Memories were her undoing. Pictures clung in her thoughts of old relationships. Some short, some longer, but all without love, without thought, without emotion. Her past suffocated her hope for a better life. Shame and guilt piled on self-loathing until she could no longer identify the motivation that guided her behavior years ago. Had she wanted to get even? If so, with whom? Her family didn't care what she did as long as she made no demands of them and fended for herself.

Today she'd wounded a man who had tried to be kind. He'd offered her a job training his dog, but he would have settled for her walking Nessie. Such a small request for such an unkind response. She needed to get a grip on life. Bogging herself down with past mistakes was stupid and went against the faith she tried to cling to even though it was difficult sometimes. Lay your burdens at Jesus' feet, and He would carry them. She shook her head, realizing how often she promised to give the Lord her troubles yet she held on as if she feared losing them.

Had they become her identity? The thought smacked her chest, knocking the little air she had from her lungs. People punished themselves in strange ways. Was holding on to her past degradation a means to destroy her chance for a tomorrow?

Weight pressed against her shoulders until her back bent with regret. She needed someone. Distraction. Anything to take her mind off her actions. Before she reached her apartment, Emily pulled to the curb and eyed her watch. Molly should have left for home by now, but Steph might still be at the shelter. She grasped her cell phone, then changed her mind. She pulled back onto the highway and headed for Time for Paws.

When she pulled through the high wire gate, Emily slowed. She shouldn't have arrived without calling first. Once there, Steph would make time for her whether she had extra time or not. She nosed her car into a space and then backed up again to make her escape, but before she pulled away, the side door opened and Steph strode outside. She lifted her arm in a wave while a questioning look filled her face.

Emily rolled down her window as Steph hurried toward her.

"What are you doing here? Dee's working alone tonight, I thought."

Dee may have been her better choice. She'd started working at Time for Paws during Steph's pregnancy. Both Steph and Molly had a way of probing too deeply.

"How are you feeling?" Emily sidestepped her question without telling a lie.

"Don't tell me you dropped by to find out how I'm doing?" She reached through the window and gave Emily a one-armed hug, then stepped back and turned in a circle. "Look at me. I've felt pretty good the past couple of days."

"Great." Emily let the car roll backward an inch. "I don't want to keep you."

Steph shook her head. "Does anything keep me when I don't want to be kept?"

A chuckle shot from Emily. It was what she needed.

Steph's eyes brightened. "I'm going shopping. Come with me."

"Shopping?" Steph knew her too well. She'd already spotted the stress on her face, and she could picture Steph having her push the grocery basket while she tried to lift Emily's spirits. "Naw. I'll see you tom—"

"What do you mean no? It's baby things. Brent keeps telling me to register for the baby shower."

Emily's resistance faded. "You know how to tempt me."

Steph held up a finger and hurried around the back of the car. The passenger door swung open. "You drive. That'll give me a break."

"Happy to. Which way?"

"Head toward Rochester Hills. I want to look at nursery furniture." She slipped in, pulled the door closed, and leaned against the seat, her hand pressing against her rounded belly. "I felt a kick." Steph turned, her eyes sparkling. "It's an amazing feeling."

Emily's heart compressed with longing. She would never marry. She couldn't, not with all she would have to confess. She dug deep to respond. "Motherhood looks beautiful on you."

Steph released a sigh. "Wait until you go through this. I'm not always beautiful, as you put it. Not with my head in the porcelain bowl. I'm grateful that's past."

Emily managed another grin and pulled out of the parking lot, distracted by their conversation. Being a mother and wife topped many women's list, but Emily avoided making any list. She'd learned to let her life happen. God had a plan for her. Some people called it a purpose, and she waited to learn what the Lord had in mind. God could do a much better job than she could in making things right in her life.

Steph filled the next minutes with conversation about items she needed for the baby, decorating the nursery, and Nick's excitement. Emily nodded and smiled at the right times, wishing she could subdue the loneliness that filled her as she lived vicariously through Steph. By the time they arrived at the store, Emily felt already drained of energy.

When she slipped from the car, Steph stood near the trunk, waiting for her, a questioning look spreading across her face. "Something's wrong?"

"I'm okay." So much for distraction. She hadn't allowed her mind to follow the joy of Steph's anticipation. Instead she'd wallowed in her own grief. "Let's pick out baby furniture. What style?"

Although Steph linked arms with her, the expression of concern didn't leave her face. "I'm not sure. Practical and pretty will suit me fine."

Emily grinned as they headed through the door, pushing back her confusion and the juxtaposition of emotions that wavered through her. Happy for Steph. Regret for herself. The pit of her stomach weighted with remorse.

Steph stood a moment to study the overhead signs, then headed into the vast display while Emily hung back, trying to deal with unwanted sensations of envy.

"Look." Steph hurried forward and stopped. "A mission-style cradle. I love it." She touched the side and the crib gave a gentle rock.

Emily touched the side, picturing a tiny sleeping newborn. When she looked up, Steph held a woven carrier.

"It's called a Moses basket." Steph held it up, showing the white lining adorned with sage-colored ribbon, but she spun away and headed down the next aisle.

When Emily caught up with her, Steph had stopped looking at the furniture but stared at her.

"Something's wrong, and don't tell me there isn't, because I know you too well."

Emily blinked, hoping to keep tears from flooding her eyes. "It's not important." She motioned toward the cribs ahead. "Let's keep looking."

Steph stood a moment, then shook her head. "No." She beckoned to her. "Let's do something else first." She turned her back and headed for the exit.

With her mind reeling, Emily watched Steph march toward the door not knowing what to do. If she'd hidden her emotions, things would have worked out better, but now she'd messed up the evening. Laying her problems on Steph, of all people, was plain old ridiculous. Martin was her brother-in-law. What could she say that wouldn't put Steph in the middle?

"Steph." She ran after her, hoping to catch her before she sailed through the doorway. Her hope sank as the door opened ahead of her, and Steph's blond hair swayed against her shoulders as she stepped outside.

Stupid. Stupid. Stupid. Emily charged through the

doorway and caught up with her. "We came here to shop, Steph. Please don't leave because of me. You're feeling good today and—"

"And hopefully I'll feel good tomorrow." She flung her arms sideways. "Or even later. We need to talk." She motioned down the street. "There's a Starbucks a block or so from here. I could use a snack, anyway."

Emily dropped her pleading. When Steph got something in her head, giving up was the best way to survive. She trotted along beside her, noticing her hand resting beneath the bulge of her belly.

After half a block, Steph glanced at her. "I'm your coworker but I'm also your friend. Friends are supposed to help friends. That's what I want to do. I'm afraid I know what's bothering you."

Hairs prickled on the back of Emily's neck. "You do?"

Steph nodded. "Baby furniture."

Emily blinked, not knowing whether to be relieved or truthful. She went for truthful. "That's part of it."

Steph glanced her way again. "I realized once we were in the store that I'd made a mistake. Two really. I wanted to kick myself when I said wait until you go through this. I know you've said so many times you'll never marry. I still don't understand why you feel that way exactly, but dragging you to look at baby furniture wasn't thoughtful of me at all."

Emily touched her arm and stopped her. "It was thoughtful. I needed to do something different, and you cared enough to invite me to join you, Steph. Maybe you don't realize that I don't make friends easily."

"Because of your—" she jerked her head toward Emily's hands "—wrists."

Her words were a statement, and Emily didn't want to correct her, but it was so much more than that. "That's the outward symbol of my desperation. I don't want to lay that on anyone's doorstep."

Steph slipped her arm around her. "You can lay your problems at my doorstep anytime. Never forget it."

Silence settled between them as Emily pondered all the baggage she lugged around. *Lay it at Jesus' feet, not Steph's,* were the words that spun in her mind. The solution sounded easy, but doing it made it too difficult.

The coffee shop came into view, and they stepped inside, placing their order, then finding a seat. Emily took a sip of her cinnamon skinny latte. She could enjoy it guilt-free, knowing it had fewer calories, although she didn't need to worry about that. Recently she'd lost a couple of pounds, and her clothes felt looser than ever.

Steph ate a bite of her pastry followed by a sip of her white chocolate mocha. "I know this sounds odd coming from me, a new Christian, but you've been a believer longer than me, and you know that God washed your slate clean. He doesn't see your sin because He sees your repentance."

Emily's gaze slipped to her wrists. She turned her hands over, revealing the evidence. "But I see these scars, and it's hard to forget. If they went away, I might feel forgiven."

"Forgiveness wraps around your heart and covers everything else, Emily. You love dogs, and you know when they do wrong you're angry at the deed, but you still love them. You forgive and move on. Look at Martin."

Emily's pulse skipped.

"Nessie ate his expensive leather belt and the handle of his attaché case. He still loves the dog. Now if he can forgive, then you know that you can forgive, too, and God is greater than we can understand. He is almighty. When He forgives, it is forgiven indeed."

Lifting her coffee, Steph cocked her head and reached across the table, tilting Emily's chin. "Are you flushing?"

"Me? No. Why would I flush?" Her heart thudded against her breastbone.

"Martin. So that's your problem. What did he do?"

She flung her hand upward, trying to stop the conversation. Any hope of opening up to Steph had faded when she'd rethought the whole idea. Sister-in-law. Brother-in-law. It just didn't work.

"He's done nothing. Really."

Steph lowered her hand and leaned back as she rolled her eyes. "Nothing doesn't make you flush, but I know he can get under people's skin."

He'd done that all right, but not in the way Steph meant it. He'd also burrowed into her dreams and thoughts. "He grates on my nerves occasionally, but he's okay."

"Really? Then you took the dog-walking job?"

Pulse kicked up again. "No. I—I—"

Steph drew in a deep breath. "What's going on? Molly said you went to Martin's house and bought dog toys for Nessie."

"I did, but I didn't stay." Time to be truthful, brother-in-law or no brother-in-law. Emily tried to explain her feelings although Steph's probing eyes caused her to muddle her words.

"You like him." Steph's eyes widened.

"No. I— Yes, he's kind, and he can be very sweet at times, but it's too hard for me to be with him."

"I would never have seen that coming." Steph leaned forward. "Don't get your hopes up."

"My hopes?" But she had, even though she'd struggle to remain realistic. He represented more than she could ever dream. "What do you mean?"

"Martin's not the marrying kind. He—"

"Marrying kind. Neither am I, and that's the problem. If my life had been different, Martin's the kind of man that any woman would hope for. I know he sometimes has an attitude, but beneath that I see a kind man who loves animals and his family. Who couldn't fall in love with that? And besides he has a good job, he's stable, and he…" Steph's look hadn't changed.

"Martin doesn't date, and he's not marriage material so any woman looking for that is barking up the wrong tree." Her expression softened as a grin grew on her mouth. "Couldn't help myself on that cliché."

Emily managed to smile back. "We're…sort of friends. That works for me." She'd longed for companionship without worrying about baring her soul. Steph's comments swirled in her mind. She lifted her cup and took another sip of the latte. Maybe she and Martin could be real friends if she could control her unexpected feelings for him.

Anyone who loved dogs captured her heart. Maybe that was all her feelings for Martin were. They both loved dogs. That was connection enough. Silly she didn't think of that before.

"What's the problem?"

Martin's head jerked up hearing Mike Schumer's voice. Mike leaned against the door frame as if he'd been waiting to catch a bus. Martin wondered how long he'd been standing there. He straightened his back. "Just thinking."

"You've done a lot of that lately." The older man pulled his shoulder from the molding and slipped his hands into his pockets as he ambled into Martin's office. He stood behind the chair in front of his desk and eyed him.

"It's not work-related if you're worried. You'd be the first person to know that. You're the chief operating officer. You know the pulse of this company."

"It's not the company I'm concerned about."

Martin eyed his friend and waved him into the chair. The man had become like a father to him since his own dad had died, and like a father, he'd told Martin to drop the attitude or he'd be a lonely man. Martin had done what sons do. He didn't listen.

Mike made his way around the chair, his focus leaving Martin only for a fleeting second as he settled into the cushion. "I'm waiting."

Squirming beneath the wise man's eyes, Martin untangled his thoughts. "It's my dog."

"You said you picked up another dog, and I told you it wasn't a good decision."

Martin shook his head. "The dog's pretty good now. It's me."

A guffaw shot from Mike's throat. "I could have told you that without the dog. So what's the real problem?"

"I found a woman to help me train Nessie, but—" Martin noticed Mike's arched brow. "She's from the shelter."

"Right."

The sound of his voice made his defenses bristle. Yes, he found Emily appealing, but mostly he was curious about her. Why did she wear oversized clothes? If she were trying to hide her attractiveness, it didn't work. She needed to wear a bag over her head or, at least, hide her beguiling eyes. He eyed his watch. "Don't you have anything better to do? I pay your salary and don't forget it."

Mike shook his head with a grin. "Here's the attitude we've talked about." He chuckled. "I think I hit some kind of nerve."

Martin's cell phone played its obtrusive tune while his fingers automatically grasped the noisemaker. He shifted his attention to Mike, but Mike motioned for him to take the call. When he flipped open the lid, Emily's name struck him and he fumbled. Trying to remain in control, he pulled the phone to his ear and said hello.

Mike rose, a know-it-all-look on his face.

"One minute, please." He covered the mouthpiece. "What?"

"I have my answer." Mike turned his back and headed for the door, but before he left, he shot Martin a coy look over his shoulder. "You can tell me about her later. Maybe I can help you with your problem." He toyed with the word problem, then vanished through the doorway.

Martin caught his breath before returning to the call.

"I've given your offer some thought." Emily's soft tone held a note of apprehension. "And I'll give it a try."

He lost his voice for a second. "You will?"

"Yes, I've been dealing with…trying to organize my time…and—"

Her discomfort pulled at his own. "And you can fit us in?"

"I think it will work."

He hitched his shoulders. "Then we should talk and make some decisions."

"Okay."

He still heard her hesitancy, but he grabbed the morsel of hope. "Can we meet somewhere?" He pushed himself from the chair and gazed out the window of his office. Dark clouds hung in the distance, and gray skies rose above him. Typical April-showers-bring-May-flowers weather.

The line remained quiet.

A chill skittered down his spin. "Or you can drop by the house anytime if that's better." He closed his eyes and waited.

"I'll come to your place. I miss Nessie."

Nessie. His chest tightened. First time he'd taken a backseat for a dog. He spun away from the gloomy window and ambled toward the doorway. "What time is good for you? Tonight?" He turned and walked back the way he came. Pacing. He'd given way to that empty activity.

"I'm working late the next two evenings. How about Wednesday?"

His heart jumped. Two days away. "Wednesday's fine. Come about five. Will that work?" Plans flooded his mind. Dinner. He would show her he could make a pretty good meal.

"I'll do my best. I should go home first and—"

"Come from work. You can grab a bite here." His hand gripped the phone. Mentioning dinner would scare her away.

"I don't want to bother you."

He paced across the room, his cell phone denting his ear. "Let me decide what's a bother and what isn't."

She didn't respond, and he knew why. He'd done exactly what he didn't want to do. He'd pushed her. His heels pressed into the new Berber carpet he'd just had laid in his office as he paced across the room and back, wishing he'd learn to keep his mouth shut.

"Thanks. I'll call you if I'm going to be late."

Late? He already knew what that meant. "I'll see you on Wednesday."

He flipped closed the phone and stood in the middle of his office. She wouldn't come. He'd blown it again.

# *Chapter Five*

Emily eyed her watch. The yipping sounds of the dogs traveled through the closed door while their dinner was poured into bowls and their water containers refreshed. Molly had arrived, and Emily knew she should have left then. She was already late. All day she'd struggled with her decision. She liked Martin too much. He stayed in her thoughts without budging even when she pushed away his image. Steph had assured her he wasn't the marrying kind and neither was she, so the relationship shouldn't be a problem. But it was.

When she saw things that bothered her, she looked away to avoid seeing them, yet even in movies that guaranteed no animals were harmed, she felt the pain of the deer buckling to the ground from a rifle shot or a prairie dog trapped by a coyote. Pain followed her. She couldn't avoid the feelings in her heart. Years ago, what she deemed romance left no emotion except sadness. Today the thought of falling in love lured her yet scared her to death.

The door to the animal pens opened, and Emily glanced in that direction, expecting to see Molly. Instead

Steph walked into the office, a frown on her face. "Why are you still here? I thought you had plans."

Emily's pulse skipped. Steph seemed to know everything. She hadn't mentioned Martin at all. "I'm leaving. It's not an appointment."

Steph walked closer. "But it's hard to keep dinner warm."

Air rushed from her lungs. "Dinner?"

Steph drew back, her frown deepening. "I thought Martin invited you to dinner."

"Martin?" Emily's heart constricted.

Steph nodded.

"I'm supposed to stop by so we can talk. He mentioned a snack."

Steph covered her face with her hands. "I'm sorry, Emily. I ruined the surprise."

Emily clung to the office desk. "Surprise? I don't understand."

"He called me a while ago and asked how to make applesauce."

"Martin's making applesauce?" Her mind tried to deal with the information.

"It's something for dessert, I think." Steph shrugged. "I don't know, but I assumed he'd invited you."

Emily shook her head. "No. Not me. It must be for someone else."

Steph shrugged again and shook her head. "Whatever. I'm sorry I said anything. I feel like a jerk."

Emily released the desk and hurried to her side. "It's okay." She gave Steph a hug. "I'd better get moving then." She turned to the coat rack for her jacket, slipped it over her new knit top and grabbed her shoulder bag. "Tell Molly I'll see her Friday. I'm off tomorrow."

Steph gave a nod, contrition written on her face.

The damp air smacked Emily as she stepped outside. She closed the door, hearing the bell tinkle from inside and hurried to her car. She flung herself into the driver's seat and slammed the door. Dinner? Steph had to be mistaken. Her head pounded. She had to call and cancel rather than put Martin in an embarrassing position if he'd invited someone else to dinner. She reached for her cell phone, then stopped. Someone else didn't make sense. He'd offered her a bite to eat. Maybe he'd meant dessert.

She pulled her cell phone from her shoulder bag and put in his number. When he picked up, her voice caught.

"Emily." His rich baritone voice weighted with concern.

"I'm late so maybe—" She swallowed the knot in her throat. "We should make it another day."

"No." The word blasted into the line. "It's fine. Please come."

His voice had softened, and her mind muddied with her earlier pondering. "I thought perhaps you'd made other plans."

"No other plans."

Nessie's yip sounded through the line.

Martin chuckled. "Even Nessie wants you to come."

Nessie. She pictured the mop of a dog, and her heart melted. "I'll be there soon." She closed the phone and sat a moment wishing she understood herself. What did she want? She wanted his friendship but continually avoided it. Having things to look forward to were alien to her. That's why life had seemed too empty. She'd pushed people away when she realized that everyone who sought her wanted to use her. Even her parents used her to release their frustration and anger. Martin's attention reminded her that most of her life love had been impossible. The reality was hers, not his.

She turned the key in the ignition and left the parking lot with Nessie's bark ringing in her ears. The dog offered a love that demanded nothing but to be loved back. A dog's faithfulness and unconditional love gave her acceptance and assurance.

She'd learned years ago from a neighbor that God offered the same gifts, and along with that, He offered salvation—her sins washed away. It was way beyond her expectation.

Trusting friends had always been a difficult time. She found comfort with Molly and Steph who knew some of her story but didn't dig into her past for more than she was willing to give. And they never judged her. Neither did dogs. She'd convinced herself that all she needed was a pet's love.

Maybe she'd been wrong. Conversation with a dog tended to be one-sided, but she felt good finding joy in life again with the animals. For so long, happiness had drifted past her like falling leaves, beautiful yet dead. In the past year, she'd had a taste of real life, real people who shared similar interests and it had opened doors, doors she'd always kept closed. And doors she wasn't sure she ever wanted to open, since it meant revealing too much.

When Martin's house came into view, her pulse quickened. She shook her head, reminding herself to be careful. Friendships should not affect her pulse, and she wished that's what their relationship could be.

As she pulled into the driveway, Nessie's nose pressed against the front window. She recalled the low bench across the expansive pane, perfect for Nessie to watch the world. Before she hit the sidewalk, Martin opened the door and stepped onto the porch.

"Hungry?" Hands in his pockets, he watched her stride toward him.

Not wanting to sound too eager, she shrugged. "A little." Her stomach rolled without sound, letting her know it wanted food and not only a little.

"Good. I decided it was just as easy to make dinner." He waved her inside.

So it was dinner. The idea made her feel as welcome as the doormat she was standing on. The scent of something wonderful greeted her from the kitchen. "I didn't know you were preparing a meal. I'm nearly an hour late. You shouldn't have waited."

An unsettling look stole to his eyes. "I've waited for many things in my life, Emily. I'm happy you came."

His words rolled down her spine, and her legs weakened. She paused to gain composure. Before she could move forward, Nessie careened toward her and proceeded to dance around her feet. She bent to pet her, but her gaze remained on Martin. "Thanks for being so nice."

He shook his head. "It's me who should say thanks. I don't enjoy eating alone."

No one did, but she was surprised he'd admitted it. Martin surprised her often. He owned a successful business, had a loving family and a social life of some kind, she was certain, yet he felt lonely too.

Studying him with new eyes, Emily felt his hand on her arm as he led her from the foyer into the living room. The dining alcove ahead of her caught her off-guard. He'd set the table with china and a real tablecloth. In the center, he'd placed a bouquet of flowers. Though they were too big for the vase and seemed to tilt to one side, the thought touched her. "I've never seen such a lovely dining table."

"Sure you have, and I suppose you've noticed the floral arrangement. I thought maybe you could give me some help with it."

She'd never arranged flowers in her life.

"While I dish up dinner, I'll give you some scissors and maybe you can make this into an arrangement."

She nodded, her heart in her throat.

Martin carried the bouquet and vase through the kitchen door and set them on the table. "I know you like flowers."

Her chest compressed, pushing air from her lungs. She stood with her back to him, drawing in the delicious scent of the meal and staring at the bouquet. The only thing she knew about arranging flowers was cutting the stems shorter.

Martin unrolled paper towel, located the scissors and handed the items to her. She peeled away the bottom leaves and snipped off the stems, dropping them on the toweling and trying to gauge how the flowers would look in the vase. When she'd cut most of them, she dropped the greens into the water and added the colorful blooms. As she tucked them in, the arrangement began to take shape.

Behind her, Martin's footsteps faded and grew louder on the wooden floor, alerting her he was carrying their dinner into the dining area.

Her hands moved with pleasure, watching how each blossom added another dimension. It reminded her of life when it was good. Each new bud of experience added to the beauty and joy of living. Life took shape. She wished she could remember that when dark thoughts drowned her in regret. She refocused, and when she'd added the last flower, she stepped back to take a look.

"Beautiful."

Martin's voice whispered close behind her.

She spun around, her face so close to his she stumbled backward.

He caught her arm. "I didn't mean to scare you. That was fascinating. I've watched my mother put flowers in a vase. Arranging them doesn't make sense to me. Maybe it's a special gene in women."

His mother. As always, the word sparked envy followed by bad memories. "I met her briefly at the wedding. Tell me about her."

He gave her a questioning look. "My mother?"

She nodded.

"She's in an independent living facility." His eyes darkened. "That was a difficult move, but she'd had a stroke, and we couldn't see her living alone. The house was too big. She's happy there now."

Though he said it, his eyes told another story. Emily wondered if his mother wasn't happy living there or if Martin felt guilty having her live in a senior residence. Maybe it was a little of both. Her heart gave a tug. "I have access to a therapy dog and sometimes visit senior residences. The people love Tinker's visit."

"You borrow a dog?"

She nodded. "It sounds silly, doesn't it?" She began to smile, and her hand flew to her mouth as it always did.

His eyes followed her hand. "It sounds kind to me."

"Thanks." She sniffed, capturing a scent floating from the kitchen. "Talking about genes, I think you have a cooking gene. That food smells wonderful."

"You'll only know how wonderful when you taste it." He lifted the vase and captured her arm with his other hand leading her back to the dining room while Nessie pattered along beside her.

After placing the flowers in the center of the table, Martin pulled out a chair for her. She gazed at it a moment, never having experienced manners like his before. She settled into the seat, her eyes on the lovely bouquet. The room had dimmed with the setting sun, and with the daylight darkening by the minute, Martin lit the candles before he slipped into the chair. "Do you mind if I say a blessing?"

Blessing? She struggled to keep her eyes from widening. And he'd asked permission. "Not at all." She lowered her head, then realized Martin was reaching for her hand. She placed her palm in his, rattled by his touch.

He closed his fingers around hers, a firm grip, while she struggled to concentrate on his simple prayer, but when she heard her name, she focused. He'd asked the Lord to bless her for her kindness. Kindness. She'd been unkind. He must have realized.

Martin released her hand with a squeeze, and she drew hers back, afraid to look in his eyes for fear he'd see the truth. When she found the courage to look up, his gaze hung on hers.

Unable to deal with her feelings, she looked away and eyed the table spread with an amazing meal. "You made all this yourself." Her gaze swept past the serving dishes—meat in a thick sauce, a bowl of noodles, green beans with almonds, and a salad.

"I did." His grin was followed by a wink.

Her pulse raced. *Stop it.* Her pulse didn't listen. "I don't cook." Why had she admitted that?

He drew back. "You don't?" Then he chuckled. "I get it."

"No you don't." She wished she'd not opened her

mouth. "I really don't cook much at all. I don't have a real kitchen."

An uneasy expression spread over his face, and he nodded. "I forgot." He reached for the meat mixture. "This is beef Stroganoff. Grab those noodles and put some on your plate."

She did, and he served two large spoonfuls of the mixture. She added the other dishes to her plate, then finally dipped her fork in the rich sauce. The Stroganoff tasted even more wonderful than the aroma. She licked her lips to catch every bite, and when she looked up Martin was watching her. "It's excellent. Better than excellent."

"Thanks. I'm glad you like it."

She took another bite, then quieted, enjoying the setting and the company. Nessie nuzzled her leg and she shifted her feet to make room for the dog to settle between.

Martin remained silent too. He gave her an occasional look, always pleasant but once in a while a question flashed in his eyes. They were feeling their way. Emily understood that. Each cautious step moved them closer to a friendship that she'd never ever experienced with a man.

Warning signals flashed through her mind, but she managed to shove them aside and drink in the pleasure of an elegant meal in a lovely home with a man who seemed to like her for who she was and nothing more.

The silence unsettled Martin. He had always drawn into himself when he was angry, but it seemed incongruous today. He was far from angry. Yet his emotion had no definition. Pleased. Hopeful. Excited. That's the part that worried him. All he knew was Emily had gotten beneath his skin. She'd kindled feelings he'd never expected to experience again, and a new life fired his thoughts. Sitting beside her at the table, he warmed with a comfortable feeling that gave him a sense of wholeness.

Emily hadn't spoken, and he avoided disturbing her. The scratch of their forks on the china was his only distraction. When she looked up, it surprised him.

Her eyes smiled at him. "This was delicious. You're a good cook. I'd love to learn to cook like this."

A vision charged through his mind. He wanted to do things for her, help her to learn to cook, let her smile a full smile instead of covering her mouth as if she had something to hide.

She lowered her fork. "I can't eat another bite."

He couldn't either. "How about some coffee or tea in the family room?"

She released a lengthy breath. "Coffee sounds wonderful."

They had to talk, and following a good meal seemed the best time of any.

When he stood, Emily rose before he could reach her chair. She scooted back and was up like a Jack in the box, gathering the dishes faster than he could. She scurried past him, heading toward the kitchen while he grabbed a couple of the serving dishes. When he came through the doorway, Emily stood beside the sink, rinsing plates with Nessie nosing beside her, as always hoping for a scrap to fall to the floor.

Having a woman help in the kitchen stood in line with being struck by lightning. Other than Steph when she and Nick ate an occasional meal with him, women had not been part of his private life—not since Denise left.

Emily and Nessie hurried off, bringing in the final dishes. He gave up trying to talk and slipped the last of dishes into the dishwasher. No conversation was possible with the woman on a mission. He leaned back against the counter while she rinsed the last plates and put them into the machine. She looked lovely and so different. Instead of the usual oversized shirts, she wore a knit top the color of a Caribbean sea. He'd never seen her wear anything as feminine, and he struggled not to stare. "Thanks for taking care of the dishes."

She grinned, her hand rising to cover her lips before she pulled it back, looking as if she were irritated with herself.

Though he wanted to ask what she was hiding, he stopped himself. Any prying caused Emily to withdraw. He hadn't learned yet what upset her and what didn't. Instead he motioned toward the doorway to the family room, then stepped to the coffeepot. "Go ahead and relax. The coffee will only take a minute."

She hesitated before she turned and did as he'd suggested. Nessie tapped along beside her, the sound of her nails vanishing when she hit the carpet.

Martin made the coffee, aware of his heart beating in his chest. He set mugs on a small tray with condiments for the coffee, and when the pot gave its last drip, he filled the mugs and headed inside.

Emily stood at the patio doorway, gazing into the yard too dark now to really see anything except a few stars hovering above the trees. He set the tray on a table and stepped behind her, wondering where her thoughts had taken her. He knew where his thoughts headed when she came to mind, and he struggled to keep his mind clear of foolish possibilities. A bad husband didn't make good material, especially one who hadn't figured out yet what he'd done, and that's where his mind took him. Never would he have imagined that a pretty pixie like Emily could arouse his thoughts to fantasy.

He released a breath, and Emily turned her head, so close his pulse tripped up his arm. "Coffee's ready."

She nodded and shifted forward as he stepped back, afraid she'd be uneasy with his standing so close.

"I'm envious of your large yard. I'd love to own a dog, but it's not allowed at my apartment." She gave a longing look at Nessie, then knelt down and petted her coat.

"What breed would you like?"

Her slender fingers rested beneath her chin as she thought a moment. "A small terrier-type, I suppose. I'm a pushover for lap dogs."

Martin chuckled. "Suzette tried to get on my lap once. It was a picture."

Her laughter rolled through the room, a lilting laugh, and he loved the sound. "Coffee?"

Instead, she turned away and pointed to a corner near the patio door. "Nessie needs a spot to call her own. Right there would work. She'd enjoy the warmth of the sun."

His offer of coffee had sailed out the window as Nessie skittered between them, her tail wagging as if waiting for something to happen.

She turned toward the fireplace. "Over there on the right would be nice, too, especially in winter."

"But how would she know that's her spot?"

She rolled her eyes. "Because you'll put her there." She lifted her index finger. "Remember the furniture you asked about at the shelter."

The image formed in his mind.

"Did you notice the—"

"Dog beds and beanbags."

"Right. I mentioned the other day she needed her

own space. Buy a dog bed that fits her. Enough room for her to shift but something cozy so she knows it's hers." She pointed to his chair. "Like that recliner beside the fireplace. You know it's yours and I bet it fits you perfectly."

He pictured himself stretched out, his feet up. The chair was home. "I got it."

Nessie lost patience. She let out a bark, her tail picking up speed.

Martin crouched beside her and tousled her head. The fur stood up in spikes as if he'd used hair gel on it.

"And a brush for her hair. You'll need that. All girls like their hair combed."

He eyed her dark hair, remembering the streaks of auburn he'd noticed in the sunshine. He tried to picture himself brushing her hair, and soon the image became too real. He felt the cool tresses running through his fingers, the soft curls bouncing back as he released the strands. He closed his eyes and opened them, longing for the images to be gone. Instead he saw her eyes, lovely eyes that captured his senses even more. "Would you go shopping with me?"

"Shopping? You mean for Nessie."

He nodded, trying to keep his expression composed. "You know what she needs, and I can learn from you." He could learn so much. He glanced at the coffee cooling in the mugs while his heart warmed to his impossible dreams.

"Not tonight."

Her words blurted into his thoughts. "Right. Another time is fine."

She nodded. "I've given this some thought, and I'll help you a little with Nessie, but if it becomes a full-time job, you'll have to find someone else."

His heart stirred. Could he find someone who'd touched him as she had? "It's a deal." He stuck out his hand.

She placed her palm against his, and he curled his fingers around her slender hand with a firm shake, but he didn't want to let go. He feared if he did she would turn and run away again, and he would never know why. He motioned to a chair, and she eyed it for a moment before settling in.

Nessie scuffled beside her and curled at her feet using her shoe as a pillow.

She smiled at the terrier before she leaned back. For once she didn't cover her mouth.

He settled into his recliner, remembering she'd called it his cozy place, and it did fit him perfectly. Without meaning to stare, he studied her long lashes as they fluttered a moment before lowering and brushing the soft tissue below her eye.

When she looked up, her eyes filled with question. "What are you thinking?"

"I'd like us to start over again. No more running for whatever reason, and then...I'd like to be friends."

"Friends?" A faint frown wrinkled her face. "In what way?"

Her question confused him. "In the normal way. Just like we are now. You look fairly comfortable with Nessie on your shoe."

She glanced to the floor and chuckled.

"I'm in my chair where I feel at home. We just had a decent meal—"

"An excellent meal."

"Thanks." His pulse skipped. "We ate and talked, too, and to be honest, Emily, I don't have many people that I do that with."

Her eyes widened, then returned to normal. "Why not? You have everything a—"

"It's a long story. Too long." He felt his pulse pick up speed. "Nothing worth talking about, but I'm pretty much a loner. Since Nick married, I miss the camaraderie." The sound of his words didn't set well. "Not to mean I'm upset or begrudge his happiness. I'm very happy for him and Steph, but he stopped by more when he was single and added a little color to my life."

An odd expression stole across her face. "You want me to be color in your life?"

He wasn't sure if she were joking or being sarcastic. "You are color in my life. Some people think everyone has an aura. If that's so, I'd hate to see mine." He managed a faint grin. "But I'm suggesting we be friends."

She didn't respond. Her eyes shifted toward the window and she looked out into the darkness for a moment. Silence weighted his shoulders, and once again, Martin feared he'd said the wrong thing.

When she looked toward him, the distrust faded. "Being friends sounds nice." She ran her fingers through her hair. "But time will tell, don't you think. Friendship isn't something you say, it's something that you feel."

*Something you feel.* He wished he could be honest and tell her what he felt, but for the good of their relations, what was the point? Friendship seemed about all either of them could handle. "You're right."

"Good." She glanced down at Nessie. "I know Nessie's a friend. Dogs are so easy to read. People can have ulterior motives. They're harder to trust."

Ulterior motives. The comment roused his guilt, but more, the depth of her words stirred his heart. Was she talking about him or someone else? "Please trust me, Emily."

She raised her eyes, and within her deep gaze, tears glistened. "Trust is hard for me."

He'd seen something in her eyes that caused him to ache. What had happened to cause her lack of trust? That its mention could bring tears to her eyes? Would she ever trust him enough to tell him?

"Then we'll take time."

Her expression softened while his chest tightened.

# Chapter Six

Emily snapped the leash on Tinker before she let him jump from her car. The black lab wore his blue therapy vest, the heart-shaped insignia with a paw print in the center. When the dog recognized the Waltonwoods Independent Living apartments, he pulled at the leash, eager to visit the residents. Emily enjoyed making periodic visits to the center, and the outing also gave Tinker a break from his quiet life. His owner, an employee at the Humane Society, worked long hours and welcomed Emily's attention to the lab.

As she steered the dog toward the entrance, a woman, sitting on her patio beneath a second story balcony, rose and headed toward her. Her cane clicked against the concrete sidewalk. Tinker stopped beside Emily, his tail working as fast as a windshield wiper in a rainstorm.

The woman smiled as she drew closer. "That's a lovely dog."

"Thank you. He enjoys coming here."

"I noticed his vest." She placed her weight against the cane. "May I pet him?"

She nodded, and the woman leaned down and drew

her hand along the dog's short coat, his tail still busy wagging while the rest of him stood still. The lab understood his job.

"His name is Tinker." Emily held the leash tightly, worried the dog's sudden move might trip the elderly lady who she guessed was recovering from a stroke. Her mouth pulled slightly to the side. Even then, she was an attractive woman.

She straightened. "Cute name. My son owns a new dog. I haven't seen it yet but I hope to soon."

"I'm sure you will."

The woman's expression looked more dubious than Emily had expected. As she studied the woman, a thought crept into her mind. "What kind of dog is it?"

"A small one. Terrier, I think. He called her Nessie."

Nessie. Emily's heart skipped. "You're Mrs. Davis."

"Why, yes." She contemplated Emily's face a moment, then grinned. "You're Emily, the sweet young lady from the dog shelter. I met you at my son's wedding." She paused a moment, her eyes searching Emily's. "And you know my son Martin, I've heard."

Her look unsettled Emily. "Yes, I know him, too." Tinker gave a jerk on his leash, apparently ready to go inside the residence.

"Call me Julia, please." She motioned to the chairs near her patio door. "Do you have time to sit?"

Julia looked eager for company, and Emily's heart tugged at the lonely look in her eyes.

"For just a moment." Emily took a step toward her porch.

"A moment's fine." She moved ahead while Emily held back wanting to give room between Julia and Tinker.

Julia motioned to a chair, and Emily settled into it while Tinker sat beside her. A Bible lay open on her seat, and Julia lifted it before settling beside her. She marked her spot and placed the Bible on her lap. "I enjoy reading out here. Inside I feel alone, but outside I can see people and the surroundings. I'm so pleased spring weather is here."

The warm April weather bolstered Emily's spirit, and so did meeting Julia. "You look well since the stroke. Much different from the wedding."

She grinned. "God is good. I was discouraged, but here I am nearly good as new."

But lonely. Emily saw that in her eyes and heard it in her voice. "I've tried to help Martin with Nessie."

Julia's gaze swept over her as a grin grew on her face. "He needs help. Martin gave up on Suzette, and I was surprised when he adopted another dog. Sometimes he doesn't accept his impatience."

Impatience. That's an attribute Emily had seen in Martin. He wanted everything perfect immediately.

"If you know my son, then you understand. He's a good boy. Martin visits me even more than Nick, but then I suppose I wasn't the best mother."

The admission charged through Emily's mind. "Why would you say that? Martin has spoken very kindly of you."

Her head jolted upward as if she'd given the woman new information. "My husband demanded a lot from the boys and me. His work and the social events that came with owning a business took my time, and then I was active in church. I tried to be a good mother, but I think I failed."

Emily hesitated, not knowing how to respond. She didn't know anything about Julia other than that she could arrange flowers. Martin had mentioned her the other day. "You raised two capable sons, Julia. Both own their own companies and are good men. You must have done something right."

"I tried. I did that, but I never gave them much rope. Their father demanded perfection from Martin. He didn't have much time to be a little boy. He wanted to please us, and that wasn't easy. His dad didn't accept mediocrity. I think sometimes that's Martin's problem. He doesn't know how to stop trying and just relax."

Her comment struck a chord with Emily. "Have you ever told him that?"

Julia shook her head. "It's too late now. Years have passed since then."

But Martin hadn't forgotten, Emily was certain. She'd watched him try too hard, and she'd seen him give up, and now she understood why. If he couldn't succeed, he didn't want to do it at all. He needed to learn to fail gracefully and to laugh at it. She needed to lighten up, too. "Martin's doing better with Nessie than he did with Suzette. She's smaller, and I suppose that helps a little."

"He's a proud man and asking for help isn't usual for him. Thank you for being his friend."

Proud? Yes, he was. And friend? Her pulse gave a kick. "I enjoy working with him and the dog." Martin wasn't the only one who needed to break out of his shell. Emily rose and signaled Tinker to her side. "We'd better get inside. It was nice to see you, Julia." She said goodbye and started down the sidewalk, but something made her pause. "I'll stop by to see you again sometime."

"That would be nice." A grin lit Julia's face, and she gave a little wave before opening her Bible.

Emily turned toward the entrance of the residences,

pondering the information she'd learned about Martin. One day it might answer questions about him. With Martin on her mind, she eyed her watch as another idea formed.

The residents greeted Tinker with the usual enthusiasm, and Emily spent forty minutes there before tearing herself away from Tinker's fans. Since the talk with Julia, her mind had drifted from her purpose, and though the dog's excitement remained, hers had flagged.

Outside she let Tinker jump into the backseat, and she slid into the driver's seat, then once again checked her watch. She still had time to call Martin. He hadn't talked with her since Wednesday, but she knew they were both being cautious. One step at a time.

Emily opened her shoulder bag and pulled out her cell phone, but before she dialed, her phone rang. She eyed the caller ID. Martin. Her stomach flipped. Coincidence or Providence? It didn't matter. He'd called her. She answered, and when he said her name something warm stirred inside her.

"I called you at home first. I thought you'd be there. You mentioned you weren't working Saturday."

"I was visiting Waltonwoods with Tinker."

"Waltonwoods. My mom lives at the one on Walton Boulevard."

She grinned. "I know. I talked with her." Her heart gave a tug.

"Hmm? How did that happen?"

"I'll tell you later. I'd thought about calling you to see if today is a good day to do that shopping you asked me about."

"That's why I'm calling."

She tilted her head back and smiled. Two minds

thinking alike. "I'll see you in a few minutes. I'll drop Tinker off on the way."

When the call ended, she dropped the phone into her bag and backed out of the parking space. Though her mind raced with excitement, as always she asked herself what she was doing. Martin was obviously older than she was. He was wealthy, well-educated and had class. Emily knew nothing about that kind of life. She grew up poor and had little education. That didn't mean she wasn't bright. She could figure things out, but she didn't have a degree. And without that, she'd failed at finding work that paid well.

The doubts that had nailed her to loneliness rose again. Martin had said to give their friendship time. She'd have to tell him that much anyway. She couldn't pretend to be something she wasn't. Classy she wasn't, and definitely not rich.

Martin stood at the doorway like an eager puppy waiting for Emily's arrival. His mind rolled with the new feelings waking to experiences long gone from his life. The idea of a fresh relationship, one that might lead to more than friendship, charged through him.

When he saw her car, his pulse jogged, and his breathing sounded as if he'd run a mile. With his emotions out of control, Martin feared he'd begin to act like a boy experiencing his first feelings of puppy love. But he was a man, not a boy.

Emily stepped from her car and headed up the walk while he managed to work his face into a pleasant expression. He feared smiling. The giddy sensations inside him could burst in a fit of giggles like a teenager's.

"Do you want me to come in or are you ready to go?"

Emily took another step before stopping at the single porch step.

"I'm ready." When he opened the storm door, Nessie bounded to his side with a look of expectancy, her tail sweeping the air. "Not you, little lady."

Emily stepped onto the porch. "We could take her."

He didn't greet her gentle suggestion with excitement. The dog tended to be a distraction, and today he wanted to test his relationship with her alone. As well, he was anxious to talk with her about the visit with his mother. That worried him. Knowing his mom, he could only imagine what she'd told Emily.

"If you bring the leash, I think they'd let her in the store. It won't take long, and we could take her to a park."

Martin remembered how she'd suddenly grown distant at the park a week earlier. He didn't want that to happen again. Yet this time, it could be fun. He'd been tangled too long in his concerns, and today he could unhook his own leash and enjoy a sense of freedom. Emily gave him hope for the life he'd let pass him by.

He eyed Nessie tap-dancing around his feet, then gazed at Emily's optimistic face. "If you think so."

She nodded, happiness growing in her eyes.

He gave in. It made Nessie and Emily happy. The plan had changed, but he needed to learn to deal with things not always going his way. Maybe that had been a problem with Denise. The thought of her bristled his anticipation, and he sloughed it off not wanting to ruin what could be an enjoyable day.

Nessie scampered into the backseat, and Emily slid beside him in his SUV. He shut her door and climbed in. When they reached their destination, as Emily had said, he had no problem taking Nessie into the pet store.

She walked close to Emily's heel, validating that quiet firmness worked with dogs.

He searched for a dog bed as Emily had suggested, and he found the right size for Nessie. He grinned thinking of her analogy to his recliner. Emily looked at things in unique ways. People and dogs. She often compared the two, and the more he thought about it the more he realized he could learn something from Nessie. The terrier was honest and eager to please. Martin had always been honest in business, but not honest in how he felt inside. That kind of honesty knotted his comfort level.

"Here we go." Emily waved him over to see a Frisbee-type disk with a terrier's face in the center.

He eyed the toy. "I don't know if I've ever played Frisbee."

She gave him a curious look. "Really? You can learn. Dogs love to fetch." She turned and gazed at the display. "How about a ball, too." She captured his gaze. "You have thrown a ball."

He couldn't help but grin. "Once or twice."

She dropped the ball and disk into the dog bed, and while he paid, she took Nessie outside to sniff the fire hydrant.

Toting the supplies, he stepped from the building and spotted Emily walking Nessie down the sidewalk. He stopped a moment, watching with interest. She wore a top in shades of green and blue spiraled together with a wide V-neck and small sleeves that showed her thin arms. Thin but strong. He wondered how many dogs she'd had to get under control during her dog-walking job.

She grinned when she noticed him—never a smile but always that selfconscious grin.

Martin tossed the packages into the hatchback and

headed toward her. When Nessie saw him, she turned and tried to race forward, but Emily drew her back. He could hear her call out "heel." He loved Emily's spirit. She looked the most comfortable training dogs.

At the car, Emily opened the back door, unsnapped the leash and let Nessie inside. Before he could act, she opened the passenger door herself. His arms dropped to his sides. His mom had taught him old-fashioned manners, but obviously Emily hadn't noticed.

He drove toward the park, aroused by memories. Nick had always walked Suzette there, and Martin had passed it many times, missing the Bouvier but happy she'd found a loving home. Nick and Steph adored the dog, not to mention Fred, Steph's border collie. The two dogs had found a kinship, pressed nose to nose at the fence when he'd become Steph's neighbor. Fred had fallen for Suzette in the blink of an eye.

Fallen for her. Another comparison. Isn't that what he'd done with Emily. Hearing the truth boggled his mind. He slowed and pulled the SUV to the grass.

Emily jumped out, grasped Nessie's leash and snapped it on. "Bring the ball or the disk."

When he opened the hatchback, to be safe, he pulled out both items and followed her. Her auburn hair looked burnished in the sunlight. The wavy strands brushed against her shoulders, and his fingers tingled to run through her silky tresses.

The unusual April warmth cooled when they stepped onto the park lawn. A canopy of elms and maples shaded the area and turned the spring grass from the color of a lime peel to forest green. He headed for a picnic table where he discarded the ball and disk, then stood and watched Emily as she clung to Nessie's leash, a question on her face.

"Does she come when you call?"

"So far. She's usually pretty good when she hears her name."

"Stand over there, and I'll drop the leash so we can see how she does in the park. Some dogs get overexcited with the freedom."

Overexcited. Martin wound his mind around the thought while he did as she asked, hoping Nessie behaved. Emily dropped the leash, and Nessie headed for him without a look sideways.

"Good girl." He patted her head, amazed she'd learned so much in such a short time.

"Ball or disk? Which are you most comfortable with?"

He gazed at her eager expression and her beautiful, shining wide-set eyes. "What difference? We're throwing it to Nessie." He closed the distance between them.

"I thought we could play, too."

The girlish look on her face stirred him. He wrapped his arms around her shoulders and gave her a hug. His action surprised him as much as her, especially since she didn't draw away. Instead he edged back, trying to be casual, while she studied him.

To cover his unexpected uneasiness, he clapped his hands. "Let's go."

Emily unhooked the leash, tossed it on the picnic table while he grabbed the disk. Nessie sensed something was about to happen. She bounded around their feet, her tongue peeking from her mouth and her eyes following the toy.

Martin ran backward, and Emily tossed him the disk. Nessie ran to him, leaping in the air like a puppy. He laughed aloud, seeing the dog's playfulness. Martin flipped the sphere to Emily, and this time, she loped it toward Nessie. The dog missed, but that didn't stop her. She snatched it from the ground and ran.

Martin and Emily both chased the dog, dodging and veering, their laughter filling the air. Finally Emily dove for the disk, tripped and skidded to the ground. Martin raced toward her as she bolted to a sitting position, her legs sprawled in front of her while Nessie leaped on her and dropped the disk into her lap.

Relieved she wasn't hurt, Martin reached for her and hoisted her up, as she laughed as cheerily as a child on a swing. For the first time, he saw it. On one side of her straight white teeth, she had a slightly crooked one. He liked the bit of character it added to her smile. No one was perfect, although he'd spent his life trying to be.

Martin stood in front of her and grasped her elbows. "Are you okay?"

"Nothing wounded but my pride." She glanced down at her grass-stained pants.

He slipped his arm round her shoulders while Nessie tried to jump up his leg. "You landed like a champ."

The dog wasn't planning to give up. So they separated again, tossing the disk, and later switched to the ball. That seemed to work better. Nessie came back to them with the ball.

Martin felt like a kid. He hadn't played or laughed as much in years, and he wished he hadn't waited so long. Life had become one serious situation after another. Maybe he was the downer and not life. Whichever, Emily had brought a new fervor to his world, and he loved the feeling.

When Nessie finally seemed worn out, Martin sat on the picnic bench with Emily beside him and Nessie safely back on the leash. His accelerated heartbeat from the exercise heightened when he looked at her creamy skin that had picked up a sunny glow.

Emily lowered her eyes and when she raised them, she grinned. "You wanted me to tell you about visiting your mom today."

His chest tightened; he was happy he didn't have to introduce the topic. "I'm curious."

She told him the story, but when she finished, Martin knew nothing about their conversation. He longed to blurt out the comment, but he stifled the urge.

Emily remained silent, then turned his head and captured his gaze. "Did you think your mom was a bad mother?"

His head lashed back. "A bad mother?" The question tripped across his thoughts, sorting out the multitude of feelings he'd had as a boy. "No, not bad."

"Then what?" A frown darkened her face.

"Not there for me. My dad was worse. Work came first, and then his social connections. That was business too, I suppose." When he said the words, they sounded cruel. His mother had changed over the years. "After my father died and I was an adult with my own business, I understood."

Her gaze probed his.

"It's hard to explain, Emily." He told her about his father's life and expectations of everyone, including his mother. "And she spent time at church involved in the women's activities. I'm not sure what."

"Bible study, I'd guess. She was reading the Bible when I saw her."

He nodded. "Mom loves her Bible. She shames me. I don't read enough."

She touched his arm, and the warmth flooded to his heart. "Do you attend church?"

"Me?" He drew back, fearing he'd winced. "Sometimes. Not enough of that either."

Emily turned on the bench to face him. "You should pick up your mom and take her to church on Sunday." She motioned toward her feet. "And she'd like to see Nessie. She mentioned she'd never seen her and wanted to."

"Mom would like—" His tongue froze. He knew what his mom wanted. She wanted more time with her sons. She wanted to be closer to them. She wanted things he couldn't give her.

Emily eyed him with expectation. "Your mother would like what?"

He shook his head. "She'd like to go to our church, but they do have services at Waltonwoods. That's more convenient."

"For who? And it's not the same. I wish I'd had a mother who wanted to spend time with me."

The words tumbled from her mouth, and her expression told him she regretted saying it. He searched her eyes, wanting her to tell him more about her life. Instead, he slipped her hand in his and squeezed it. "I'll take her to church soon. I promise."

"And I'll make sure you keep that promise." She squeezed back.

Her small hand in his rattled his emotions. He'd never grasped a woman since Denise or kissed her, but the desire overwhelmed him. He rose from the bench and eyed his watch. "Did you know we've been here two hours? Are you ready to go?"

She shrugged and became quiet.

They settled into the SUV, and he drove away aware that something had happened again. When he pulled into his driveway, she slipped out—this time not attempting to make it to her door—and she lifted Nessie from the backseat before he pulled into the garage. His mind raced trying to resolve the tension that always occurred. He failed.

He met her on the driveway as she fastened Nessie's leash. He took it from her hand. "It's nearly dinnertime. Would you like to stay? I can fix something."

"Thanks, but no. I really need to leave."

He stopped himself from pushing the invitation. With Emily, he'd met his match. He strode beside her as she headed to her car on the other side of the driveway. When she opened the door, he noticed a tear in the upholstery. What did he expect of a ten-year-old automobile?

Emily clasped the doorframe as if she feared he would force her into the house. "Thanks for the nice day." She slipped into the sedan and closed the door. She gave a brief wave and backed up.

Martin watched her go, taking with her a piece of his heart. As he strode inside, he tried to recall the conversation. They'd talked about his mother, but she'd introduced the topic so she couldn't blame him. And she was adamant that he take his mother to church.

Then it struck him. *I wish I'd had a mother who wanted to spend time with me.* She'd been silent about her past and her family. Yet telling him about it took trust, and trust wasn't something she had.

# Chapter Seven

"I can't get home, Emily. Could you drop by and check on Nessie? I keep a key in a rock sitting in the shrubs beside the porch."

Emily pulled her cell phone away from her ear and stared at it. The past week, Martin had called twice to ask a favor. Once it included picking up his laundry before the place closed. She knew Nick had been his go-fer, as Steph called it, but she didn't plan to be.

Though she didn't like the idea, her heart wanted to agree, but her head told her she was enabling his old rut. "I have a number of jobs myself tonight. I'm not sure I can make it."

"If you can, I'd appreciate it. I really can't get away early, and I know how hard it is on Nessie."

Emily's conviction weakened.

"She's been very good, and—"

"I'll see what I can do. That's all I'll promise." But she knew she'd be there. Somehow Martin had been able to pull her strings, and she'd tried to rein them in with the same technique she learned to train dogs...except dogs listened. She didn't.

He thanked her and promised to not bug her again, but he'd said that before. She hung up, realizing that if he kept on asking her to take care of his responsibilities she would become another of his flunkies. He would end up not respecting her, and she wouldn't respect herself. Things had to change. Martin needed to learn he didn't have to have everything work out the way he wanted.

She eyed the wall clock. Two of her clients had called and asked her to switch the time to later in the day, and another person called and asked if she could watch their dog while they vacationed. They wanted her to stop in two or three times each day, but mostly, they encouraged her to stay at their house while they were gone. She preferred not to. The whole thing added stress to her life, but they were willing to pay for the extra service, and she could always use the money. Since her hours at Time for Paws often shifted from morning to afternoon to evening, she tried to be flexible.

When Dee arrived at the shelter, Emily headed outside, drawing in a deep breath of spring air. Tomorrow would bring May, which meant the rainy days should fade. Warmer days promised spring flowers, and she longed for them. Clusters of grape hyacinth had made their appearance earlier when snow still dotted the ground, but recently tulips and daffodils had nosed through the earth, their buds promising colorful displays, followed by lilacs hanging from trees and flowerbeds bordered with impatiens and petunias.

Flower gardens lifted her from the gloomy days she remembered when her parents' yard moved from spring to winter with the same broken bottles, rusted tin cans, weeds and dead grass, never changing. Her life had followed the same blighted path with no change and no hope. Until now.

Today more traffic than usual sailed along Rochester Road, but she slipped into the traffic, and within an hour, she'd visited the two clients and decided to stop at Martin's before making her final stop to spend time with the Jack Russell who must miss his vacationing family. The dog made her a bit nervous. He appeared to be edgy with strangers, but the owner guaranteed her the dog was testing her. She hoped she could pass the test.

When she arrived at Martin's, Nessie sat in the window, and when she saw Emily, she bounded off the window seat, and Emily knew she was jigging at the door to get out. After she located the rock in the bushes, she opened the door and was greeted as she suspected. Nessie darted around her as if she couldn't decide whether she wanted to be petted or to get outside. Rather than clean up after the little fluff ball, Emily opened the patio door and let her out. Nessie darted across the yard as if she'd been freed from prison.

Emily stood in the doorway, feeling the sun's warm rays on her arms. Martin's house triggered her longing for a larger apartment. One day she hoped the Lord blessed her with a home where the outside was accessible. Even a small apartment on the ground floor where she had an outside entrance. Anything but being locked away in a place not much bigger than a walk-in closet.

She'd never had a full view of Martin's home, and being alone, the urge struck her. She crossed the family room and passed through the doorway to the hall that led to the other rooms. Guilt slithered up her back, thinking she should stop herself, but already she'd walked down the hallway glancing at a bedroom on the right that appeared to be used as his home office. A desk sat against the wall, and across the hall, she looked into a large room with beige carpet and walls a little darker with the bed neatly made with an earth-tone spread. The room had a masculine feel, and when she moved closer to the doorway she spotted the walk-in closet. The open door drew her closer, and as she suspected, it was about half the size of her apartment.

She backed out, forcing herself not to investigate further. As she turned, she noticed another bedroom, large enough to make any guest comfortable. Martin's mother came to mind. Julia could easily stay there for a weekend visit.

Struck by guilt, Emily hurried back to the patio door, wishing she hadn't nosed around. Martin had never offered her a tour of the house, and she should have respected that, but living in a tiny apartment as she did, the luxury of so much space aroused her curiosity. She tried to explain away her actions but faced the truth. She'd overstepped Martin's trust.

When she slid open the patio door, Nessie scampered inside, heading for her water dish. Emily refreshed it, crouched to pet her soft coat, and then rose, facing her last stop. Getting familiar with new dogs had become the least favorite part of her job.

She locked Martin's door, and, making sure no one had been watching, she returned the key to the rock and placed it into the shrubs where she'd found it. A key so close to the door made her nervous.

As she drove, her mind settled on the lovely guestroom that would suit Julia well. Martin could easily spend the weekend with her, and she plied her mind with ideas to convince Martin it would be a good idea.

The new client's house came into view, and Emily pulled into the driveway. She located the house key, repeated the dog's name to make sure she remembered, and unlocked the door. When she stepped inside, she was greeted by bared teeth and a menacing growl. She didn't move.

"Remember me, Rusty?"

The dog's growl deepened, his beady eyes staring her down.

Emily had no intention of letting a dog the size of a Jack Russell scare her away. The family was out of the state, and she had a job to do. She inched forward and stopped when Rusty's grumble turned to a snarl. Emily lifted her head upward, sending a prayer. God loved all creatures, and if He wanted the dog to be fed and cared for, maybe He could get the dog to cut her some slack.

As her mind raced, she heard her cell phone ring inside her handbag. She gazed down, fearing if she moved her hand the dog would be after her. She inched backward, and the dog charged her. Emily darted through the front door and closed it before digging into her bag. The last jingle faded when she pulled out her cell phone. She eyed the screen. Martin. Her heart leaped with relief. She hit the answer button, and when she heard his voice, she drew in a deep breath.

"Thanks for stopping by. When I realized I could get home earlier than I expected, I planned to let you know, but you'd already been here."

Air streamed from her nose and sounded against the phone.

"Emily, I'm sorry. I know I've—"

Her mind clicked. "Martin, how would you like to do me a favor?"

He hesitated, and she waited.

"What kind of favor?"

"Do you have a thick pair of work gloves, and maybe a piece of meat?"

"A what?"

She explained her predicament and was greeted by Martin's chuckle, but he finally came around. "Where are you?"

She gave him the address, then sat on the porch step waiting for his arrival. The sun had lowered in the sky, and the air became cooler. A chill rustled through her, one of frustration along with the weather. Never had she been in this position. When she'd been introduced to the dog, he hadn't been overly friendly but he'd not attacked her.

When Martin's car pulled into the driveway behind hers, she rose, surprised to feel tears in her eyes. Embarrassed by her reaction, she swiped them away and waited for him.

Approaching her, Martin's expression changed from a half grin to one of concern. He didn't speak but slipped his arms around her, and unable to control her mortifying frustration, she planted her face in his shoulder and wept. He remained silent as his hand brushed against her back, soothing her.

When she'd gotten under control, Emily lifted her head, wanting to run to her car and drive away. She felt inept and ridiculous. "I've never had this kind of problem before. Never."

His tender look touched her. "I thought you'd gone into lion taming."

The comment was said so sincerely, Emily sputtered into a chuckle. Crooked tooth or no crooked tooth, she grasped the humor in the situation.

Martin released her and approached the door. "Is the door locked?"

She nodded. He pulled the gloves from his back pocket and slipped them on his hands.

When he opened the door, Rusty waited on the other side, his growl deep and his teeth still bared, but instead of charging, he hung back.

"He's a watchdog, Emily. Use your training techniques." He glanced at her. "You let the dog bully you instead of taking command."

She lowered her gaze, realizing he was right. "Rusty," she spoke in a commanding voice. The dog growled.

"Rusty, sit."

The growl turned to a deep-throated gurgle.

"Sit."

The dog looked from Martin to her as his growl faded. Finally he sat.

Emily scurried past him into the kitchen. She opened the pantry and pulled out the dog's food. Rusty followed her through the door but stood back watching her, then edged forward. Martin grasped an oversized container and filled it with water. The dog gave the water a few laps and headed toward the back door. Emily swung it open and Rusty ran into the yard while she stood beside Martin, shaking her head. "I feel foolish."

He slipped off the gloves and tucked them into his back pocket. "You're not foolish." He tilted her chin upward. "You lost your confidence. It happens to the best of us."

Beneath his comment, Emily sensed a different meaning. Martin often said things inside out, and she had to decipher the implication. Today a look filled his eyes that Emily could read. Her pulse charged as Martin bent and kissed the end of her nose.

When he drew back, his eyes sparked with tenderness. "You're amazing."

He didn't back away and neither did she. "So are you."

Grinning, he gestured toward a kitchen chair. "Might as well be comfortable."

Pleased that he hadn't rushed off once the problem had been resolved, Emily settled into one of the chairs, and Martin joined her. As she looked at him, her mind drifted back to his house and her self-guided tour. "I toured your house today when I was there." She clasped her hands in a knot and rested them on the round maple table.

A frown slipped to his face, and she cringed. "I shouldn't have, and I'm sorry."

The expression faded, replaced by a teasing look. "My bed was made, I hope."

The comment made her grin. "It was."

"Sorry I didn't give you the five-dollar tour before. I never think anyone would want to see the place." He slipped his hand over hers. "And if we're confessing things, every time you smile without covering your mouth, it makes me happy. I never would have noticed your tooth if you hadn't made a big deal out of it. I like it. You know, mountain out of a molehill. The smile gives you character." His eyes searched hers. "I think we often take what we think are flaws and turn them into disfiguring scars. Know what I mean?"

Emily understood, but he didn't understand the depth of her problem. She wished her problems were only molehills. She studied Martin's face, longing to know even more about him than she'd learned from Julia.

Leaning against the chair, Emily pictured Julia's face. The image aroused her earlier thoughts, and no matter how Martin took it, she had to speak her mind. "Your guest room would make a nice weekend room for your mother."

The scowl returned. "You're on my mother again."

"She's lonely. You have a room she could stay in over a weekend so she feels…loved."

Martin shook his head and rose. "My mother knows she's loved. I buy her flowers."

Emily stood too, wanting to make her point. "Flowers only cost money and a couple of minutes. A visit takes caring."

He drew back, viewing her in his peripheral vision. "You don't think I care?"

"I think you care when it's convenient." She winced hearing the harsh words.

He looked away and strode to the backdoor.

She expected him to leave. He didn't. Instead, he faced her. "I don't want to discuss this."

Her eyes burned fighting tears that wanted to pool on her lashes. He didn't understand because it hadn't happened to him. As she calmed, she recalled Martin had mentioned he'd missed some of the nurturing that children needed. Even Julia had agreed.

She stepped forward and caught his arm. "Martin, forget what I said. I don't know your situation. I only know my own, and what I think comes from my experience, not yours. What I said wasn't fair."

He captured her hand beneath his, his face less tense. "Emily, I don't want to be like my parents were when I was younger. I should be a better example because I know how lonely and unloved I felt at times."

"Martin, I didn't—"

"It's okay. You've given me something to think about." He gave her hand a brief pat. "You've got things under control here." He lowered his arm and stepped back. "I need to get home." He sidestepped her and headed toward the front of the house. "Thanks for being honest about your feelings."

"But I…" The words stuck in her throat, and she let them die.

Honesty needed to be in both directions. They both had a lot to learn. She'd been far from honest with Martin, and if they were true friends, she would stop hiding her past. God saw what she'd done, and He'd forgiven her. Could Martin do the same if he knew the truth?

Emily's words rattled in Martin's head for the rest of the evening and all day Saturday. On Sunday he visited his mother, but Emily's comments ruined the visit. He felt guilty. Bringing his mother home for a Sunday dinner wouldn't hurt him at all. Why hadn't he done it before? Emily had been right. It hadn't been convenient.

Martin lowered his head, trying to concentrate on the work piled on his office desk. He had to change. His mother needed him, and she needed love in the same way he wanted it so badly as a child. He pictured his father's determined jaw. He envisioned his face when he looked into the mirror to shave. Sometimes his jaw had that same hard look, but that was before he'd made an effort to alter his ways. It was either change or expect his life to continue as it had. Lonely.

Nick had taught him a lesson without even trying. When Nick fell in love, Martin envied him to the point that he made life hard for his brother. He hadn't been pleasant to Steph, and all in the guise of protecting Suzette from Steph's dog Fred. The border collie had been no trouble except the one time he'd tried to dig a hole under the fence. Martin should have learned his lesson then. Fred wanted to make friends with Suzette. The dog was lonely.

A deep breath escaped Martin. He'd been even

lonelier. His head throbbed, and he lifted his fingers and massaged his temples. Trying to concentrate had become even worse today than yesterday. All he could picture was his mother's frail look, her gentle smile with talk of Emily's visit and waiting to meet Nessie. How simple it was to solve the problem. But he'd been stubborn, and for no reason except it was easier to be the old Martin than the one he really wanted to be.

He could be different if he would let the old behaviors go. The Bible said he was a new creation in Jesus, and the Lord had offered to carry his burdens. As he stretched his neck to relieve the tension, Martin rolled back his chair and spun around to face the window. Dark clouds billowed overhead pressing on him like a gray blanket. His office smothered him today. He turned back and picked up his pen, his focus on papers in front of him, but the pen slipped from his fingers. He needed to get outside and walk off some of his frustration.

Why not?

With relief already on the horizon, Martin stood, grabbed his suit jacket and strode into the outer office. "I'm leaving for a while."

His secretary nodded and went back to her work.

When he reached the doorway, he paused. "I don't think I'll be back today, Janet, so put everything off until tomorrow."

"No problem, Mr. Davis."

He gave her a wave and headed toward the side door. He'd told Janet numerous times she could call him Martin. She never did. He was Mr. Davis. Calling him Martin probably seemed too friendly to her. He had sometimes been unpleasant. The thought added another weight to his over-taxed mind.

He hit the remote, and his car beeped as the locks

lifted. He slipped inside and turned the key. As he backed out, a drop of rain hit the windshield and looking at the dark sky, he turned on his headlights. The drops multiplied as he pulled onto the highway. Dark days seemed to bring the worst in people. May had come and the flowers needed water, but he needed sunshine more. He turned the wiper switch, his thoughts beating back and forth in the same rhythm. Emily. His mother. His attitude. Nick's marriage. The list went on as thoughts as heavy as the falling rain barraged him.

He slowed at the stoplight, questioning his decision to leave the office. The work needed action. So did he.

Traffic moved, and Martin turned onto his street, grateful he wasn't out walking in this. Ahead he saw a pedestrian running with a dog. His heart stopped. Emily and Nessie. He tooted the horn and pulled beside her as he rolled down the passenger window. "Get in."

"No. I'm soaked."

"I can see that. Get in." He leaned across the seat and pushed open the door.

She stood a moment, rain rolling down her face and Nessie looking like a wet mop.

"Don't just stand there."

She slipped in, her clothing sticking to the upholstery. Nessie jumped in and made a dive for Martin's lap. Emily grabbed her before she did too much damage to his suit.

"Bad timing, huh?"

She gave him a blank stare.

"For the walk."

"I guess." She lowered her eyes.

He sensed her uneasiness. They needed to talk, but not while she was sopped and shaking with the chilly rain.

In moments, he pulled into the driveway and into the garage. Emily opened the door and slipped out with Nessie still in her arms. Both of them were trembling, and he hurried to the door and opened it. They stepped into the laundry room while he scooted past them. "Stay here a minute."

Martin hurried into his bedroom and grabbed a robe and some towels from the linen closet, then darted back. "Hand me Nessie, and I'll dry her off while you put on this robe."

She shook her head. "I can't do that. My clothes are sopped and I need to go home."

"You're not leaving here that way. I let you do it once, but not again. I'll shut this door, and when your wet clothes are off, toss them in the dryer, and then head to my bathroom. It has a great shower, and I'll leave some clothes for you to slip into."

"Martin, I ca—"

"Yes, you can."

He stepped into the breakfast room and closed the door. With Nessie still shivering in his arms, he headed for his bathroom, toweled the dog and then let her go while he searched through his closet for a pair of sweat pants and shirt. Martin placed them on the bathroom counter. To avoid embarrassing her, he hurried to the family room with Nessie prancing at his feet, but she slipped past him and headed for the kitchen, probably checking on Emily.

A chill had settled in the room, and Martin leaned over and lit the gas fireplace, so real-looking no one could believe it wasn't wood burning on the grates. In his peripheral vision, he saw a blur dash past the door. He slipped into the kitchen, turned on the burner and grabbed the tea kettle. From the laundry room, he heard the sound of the dryer, and he felt relieved that for once she'd listened to him.

After filling the pot, Martin put it on the burner and looked into his pantry for tea bags. He spotted a package of scones and grabbed them along with jars of marmalade and butter. By the time he heard Emily speaking to Nessie rustling around the family room, the tray was ready.

When he came through the doorway, she looked up, surprise filling her face. "You didn't have to do that."

"I wanted to." He set it on a low table in front of the fireplace. "Feels good, doesn't it?"

She nodded, noticeably uncomfortable in his clothing. Instead of makeup, her face glowed from the fresh shower. Her hair had already begun to dry from the heat of the fireplace. Martin grasped the teapot. "I hope you like tea."

"I do. Just black." She watched as he poured tea into the cup. "Are those biscuits?"

"Scones. I like them with marmalade especially." He didn't wait for her response, but buttered one and added a swirl of the marmalade. When he offered her the plate, she took it and turned to the fire.

In the dimmed light from the storm, firelight danced on the floor. Emily watched the flames as if she'd never seen a fireplace before. "I can imagine how cozy it is to sit here on a winter day and enjoy the fire." She glanced his way. "It feels good."

"You were shivering when I picked you up on the road." He sat across from her, unable to take his eyes from her as she sat so close looking like she belonged there. Her mention of cold winter nights sent his imagination flying.

She became silent as she reached for the tea. She took a sip and leaned back, her gaze on the flames.

He let the hush linger though he had so much to say. But sometimes quiet was better than words.

"This was kind of you." She shifted in the chair and focused on him.

Her eyes said so much Martin couldn't take it all in. "I might be a jerk sometimes, but I wouldn't let you go home in those wet clothes. I'd never forgive myself."

She lowered her eyes.

"Anyway, you look better in my sweats than I do."

A faint smile crept across her face. "I thought you were upset with me the other day, and I felt so—"

"No. You're wrong. I was angry at myself. I've given a lot of thought to what you said about doing things when they're convenient. I've done a lot of thinking the past few days, and you're right, I don't know how difficult your life was. I don't know much about you at all, but I'd like to."

Panic swept across her face.

"But only when you're ready...if that might ever happen." He leaned closer, resting his elbows on his knees. "I've been dragging old baggage around, too, Emily, and it's time I admit it and toss it into that fire there."

Her gaze drifted to the fire, and the light shimmered across her hair, adding mahogany highlights to her dark brown strands. Martin's fingers yearned to touch the slight curl that had formed when it dried.

"I visited my mom on Sunday."

She turned toward him, her expression questioning.

"She wants to see Nessie. I should have done that long ago, and Mom's lonely. I know that." He rose and stood beside her. "You were right. I do things out of convenience. I don't think of others at times. I ask you to run my errands, and—" He knelt beside her. "You do. It's your nature to be thoughtful."

"I don't always want to be."

Her decisive look threw him a curve. "But you do. Why?"

Her expression softened. "It's how I wish I would be treated. That was one thing I learned from a woman in the apartment across from mine who told me about Jesus and gave me a Bible. I read the New Testament first, and something Jesus said struck me. 'Do to others as you would have them do to you.' I never learned that at home. It's been a good lesson for me."

Martin winced at the sadness in her voice. "That's a lesson for everyone. I guess it's what I said earlier. I do things when it's convenient, but I expect people to jump." A thread of guilt wove through his conscience. "I should be doing the jumping too."

She ran her fingers through her hair. "It's drying, and my clothes should be, too. I need to go."

He rose and offered her his hand. She stood, looking so small and delicate swimming in his large clothes. "I'm going to bring my mom home next weekend if she'll come."

A smile grew on her face. "What do you mean if?" She touched his arm. "She'll love to."

"I'm afraid we'll sit there after an hour and have nothing to say. I guess that's what I dread."

She shook her head. "Martin, conversation is natural, and silence can be golden. Your mother doesn't need to be entertained. She needs to be loved."

Her words punched his heart.

She turned and headed to the kitchen door.

"Emily?"

She turned around.

"Would you come on Saturday for dinner? I think Mom would like it." An earlier idea spiraled into his mind. "Come early and you can help me."

She cocked her head, a faint scowl on her face. "I don't cook. I told you."

"You will when I get through with you."

She chuckled. "I suppose I can do it for your mother."

"Thanks. She'll be pleased, and I'll be even happier"

She looked at him a moment, searching his eyes, then turned and headed into the utility room. He stood there, already feeling lonely and realizing he needed to be loved, too.

# Chapter Eight

Although Martin had offered to pick her up, Emily thought it was silly and refused his offer. She couldn't get accustomed to his polite manners, although she liked them. He treated her like a woman who deserved respect. She struggled with that.

Emily searched her clothing for something to wear. She wanted to wear something casual, but most of those outfits she wore at work. The best thing about the new job with Rusty was she often slept in the owner's house, and she enjoyed the larger income it brought in from her once-a-day walks with the dogs. The new job had started out a catastrophe, but Rusty and she had become friendly, although she couldn't forget those bared teeth. Hopefully with the extra income from this job, she could shop for a few new outfits.

Finally she selected a pair of black pants with a black and white knit top. Then to make herself feel more spring-like, she pulled out the yellow blazer she'd purchased to wear at Steph's wedding with her new dress. After brushing color on her cheeks and brightening her mouth with lipstick, she slipped on the jacket and left, her pulse zinging with anticipation of spending the day with Martin and his mother. A family. The image heightened her excitement. As always, the fear of being hurt never left her mind.

As Emily drove down Martin's street, her hands fidgeted against the steering wheel, and when she pulled into his driveway, her anxiety grew. She sat a moment to calm herself. In the window, she spotted Nessie jumping off and on the seat, and when she opened her door, she could hear her high-pitched barks coming through the window.

The unseasonably warm weather touched her senses. Growth and newness sprouted around her, and somewhere inside a hope needled her to join nature and grow too. She grinned, watching Nessie's animated greeting. Honesty. She knew the dog loved her. The feeling was mutual.

By the time she reached the door, Martin stood there waiting for her. His gaze swept over her as a grin stole to his face. "You look amazing. You look like spring."

A flush warmed her cheeks. "Thanks."

He pushed open the door, and she stepped into the cool foyer. Air conditioning. She had one in her bedroom window and another in the living room. Neither was effective. But this was a new day, and Martin had become a friend. His eyes sparkled with welcome, and she felt at home for once. He'd worn jeans again with a maroon knit pullover, and the color highlighted his dark hair and a faint shadow of whiskers added to his classic good looks. She drew in a breath, amazed she was standing in his foyer.

When Emily strode forward, her gaze swept the living room, looking for his mother. She started to ask when she heard his mother's voice from the family room.

"It's Emily, Mom." Martin grinned at her. "She's been waiting for you. I think she looked forward to your coming more than staying here for the weekend."

She waved away his words and strode ahead into the family room.

His mother stood beside a chair, her Bible resting on a nearby table and a magazine lapping over the chair arm. "There you are."

"It's so nice to see you again." Emily hurried to her side and, without thinking, kissed her cheek. She backed up too embarrassed to look at Julia.

"You are a dear." Julia's voice sounded warm and pleasant as if nothing unusual had occurred.

With the dog prancing around her feet, Emily used the distraction to get a grip. "What do you think of Nessie?"

Julia resettled into the chair and expounded on Nessie while Emily slipped off her jacket and listened to Martin working in the kitchen, hopeful he'd given up on the idea of her helping prepare dinner. She nestled into the chair, adding comments when Julia slowed to take a breath. Though she didn't know her well, Emily recognized Julia's excitement at being in Martin's home. The awareness saddened her, and she hoped Martin had learned something from their conversation although she worried she'd said too much.

Julia became silent for a moment, then reached to pick up the Bible. "Do you read Scripture?"

The question smacked Emily. "I'm a Christian, but I don't read much."

"The Bible has been my solace as I've grown older. I was neglectful when I was your age, too. I'm grateful both my boys are believers. We did something right."

"You did many things right, I'd say."

Julia's face brightened. "Thank you, Emily." She leaned back, placing the Bible on her lap. "Martin's taking me to church in the morning. Would you like to join us?"

The invitation had been unexpected, and Emily knew she could come up with a million reasons why she couldn't, but the look in Julia's eyes pushed away all her excuses. "That would be nice. Thank you for asking."

Julia clapped her hands together, a crooked smile growing on her face. "Wonderful. I'm pleased."

"Ready to give me a hand?" Martin's voice floated in from the kitchen doorway.

Emily caught her breath. Two invitations within seconds, but one she wanted to avoid. Cooking. Her hope that he'd changed his mind fizzled. "What about keeping your mother company?" She tossed out her last piece of ammunition. "I'll stay—"

"You go right ahead." Julia responded before Martin had a chance. "My eyes are getting tired, and I might just take a little nap."

Martin strode into the room, giving Emily a look that defied her comprehension. Then he focused on Julia. "Mom, sit in the recliner. You can lean back and rest."

Julia eyed the chair and nodded. "I think I will." She rose and made the few steps to Martin's favorite chair without her cane and settled in.

Martin helped her tilt back the recliner, then beckoned Emily to follow.

She rose, stuck with showing her ineptness in the kitchen.

When she came through the doorway, he tilted his head and studied her. "Did I hear my mother ask you to go to church with us?"

Ah-ha. That explained the look she didn't understand. "She did, and I accepted."

"But you don't want to." His eyes searched hers with question.

"No, I'm happy to go."

Tension eased from his face. "I'd love you to join us, but don't let her pressure—"

She rested her hand against his cheek. "It pleased her that I said yes." She grasped her courage. "What I don't want to do is this."

He gestured toward the kitchen counter. "You mean help with dinner."

"I'm willing to help with dinner, but I'm not a cook."

"And you'll never be if you don't learn." He stepped toward her and slipped his arm around her shoulder. "You've been my teacher with Nessie. I knew nothing about training a dog in obedience. Now it's my turn to show you a few things. Fair is fair."

She gazed up at him, a knot in her throat. "I suppose if you put it that way." She loved the feeling of his embrace, but it only reminded her of how impossible their relationship seemed. She had nothing more to give than what she had already given him—her knowledge of training a dog.

He drew her so close, she could hear him breathing against her hair, and she felt him tremble before he kissed her hair and stepped back. His reaction addled her. She wanted to see his expression, but he'd turned away and crossed the room. Had he felt pity? Her chest tightened. She didn't want anyone's pity.

When he came toward her, he carried a cookbook and set it on the table. "I thought we'd make something with chicken. Want to look at the poultry recipes?"

Emily didn't want to look at recipes, but Martin's voice drew her to him. She sank onto a stool at the island and opened the poultry tab. She stared at the recipes without seeing them. She'd prepared hamburgers and casseroles, things her mother had thrown together when she had time. Otherwise Emily had eaten bread with cheese or meat if it had been in the house. More than once she'd eaten buttered bread with sugar sprinkled on it for her meal. Tears pushed against her eyes. She'd become part of a lush world dressed in rags with empty pockets.

"I have an idea." Martin's voice jolted her.

She looked up.

"I think I have everything we need." He opened the refrigerator and looked inside. "Let's try chicken cordon bleu."

"Chicken what?" Fried chicken. Broiled chicken. Chicken fingers she'd picked up at a fast food restaurant. Her grandmother made baked chicken for a holiday meal, she remembered.

"A fancy name for an easy meal. Trust me."

Trust. The word rustled through her.

"My mother made this meal for some of their fancy dinner parties. I have her recipe." He dug into a drawer and pulled out an index card.

Emily could see it was handwritten. Martin placed the card in front of her and took away the cookbook. She studied the ingredients—chicken breasts, Swiss cheese, ham, flour, eggs, breadcrumbs. It all sounded fine, but now he expected her to make it.

They worked side by side, and while she measured the flour and cracked the eggs, he boned the chicken breast and tossed the bones into the water for rice pilaf. She'd never eaten that, either. While Martin prepared the breadcrumbs, he assigned her the job of flattening the chicken breasts with a contraption he had in a drawer. The idea of making a dinner in this elegant kitchen seemed a dream. As she hammered the chicken breasts, Emily's gaze traveled along the expanse of counter space to the island, then across to the lovely bay window where the kitchen table offered a view of the beautiful outdoor landscape. Home. Her heart thundered.

When she'd finished, Martin showed her how to place a slice of cheese and ham onto the flattened chicken and roll it into a tight cylinder. He dipped the rolled chicken into the egg mixture, then the crumbs and placed them in the oven as the scent of chicken broth rose from the pot.

"Let's take a break." He glanced into the family room and winked. "Mom's sleeping. It's a pretty day, and Nessie's ready to go outside."

Emily followed him as they tiptoed past his mother and stepped outside. Martin gestured toward the table where they'd sat eons ago, it seemed. She settled into the same chair she'd used that day, but this time, he pulled his chair beside her. Though the sun still held warmth, she wondered if she should have brought out her jacket. A chill fluttered through her, and when she looked up Martin was watching her.

"Are you cold?"

"No. I think it's contrast from the warm kitchen."

His eyes hadn't left her, and her pulse charged along her veins. This was all too lovely. Too dreamlike. She'd longed for a good life and a husband who loved her no matter what she'd done, but dreams weren't reality, and keeping that in the forefront of her mind dampened the joy she felt in Martin's company.

"Do you mind if I ask you a question?"

His voice cut through her thoughts. Question? Yes, she minded, but... "What kind of question?"

From his expression, she sensed he witnessed her apprehension. "You don't have to answer if you don't want." He leaned closer, slipping his hand over hers as it gripped the chair arm. "You mentioned learning about Jesus from a lady who lived near you."

She nodded, waiting for what came next.

"I take it your parents weren't believers?"

"They weren't." She pictured her parents in their small house, needing so much and wasting their money on cigarettes and alcohol. Without willing herself, her mouth opened and she spewed out some of the story. "I felt different than other kids at school, and I never connected with them. When it was their birthdays, the mothers brought in cupcakes for the class to celebrate. My mother never did. I don't even think she remembered my birthdays."

Martin's concerned expression turned to a frown. "You never celebrated your birthday?" He shifted his hand and wove his fingers through hers.

The warmth of his palm spread up her arm. "When I was very young, I remember one gift. A stuffed animal. A camel-colored puppy. But never after I was eight. I tried not to think about it. May 22 escaped me like any other day. Otherwise it hurt too much." She hated confessing the pangs of sorrow she'd felt. "Don't pity me, Martin. That's worse than the experience."

His face paled. "I don't pity you. I'm astounded." He wrapped his other hand over their woven fingers.

His touch distracted her, and she drew in a deep breath. "Don't be shocked. I'm not the only child in the world who never had a birthday celebration."

He looked thoughtful, and finally nodded. "I know, but it must have been difficult growing up that way."

His tender voice riffled through her. She lowered her eyes, not wanting him to read the thoughts pounding in her mind. "I had little connection with my family. I lived there, and spent time in the little bedroom I shared with my older sister until she ran off and got married way too young. I haven't seen her in years."

Compassion filled his eyes. "That's sad. Nick and I had our bad times, but I'm grateful I have a brother."

"Nick's a great person." And to be honest, she wasn't sure it was sad about her sister. Maybe in running away she'd found a good life, and if not, adding that regret to Emily's consciousness wouldn't help a thing.

"You might think my life was perfect, but it wasn't. Yours had to be more difficult than mine, but I carried around baggage for years until recently."

She recalled things Julia had said, and a few of Martin's comments. Maybe money and success wasn't everything. "Life is hard."

"It is, but it can get better, Emily. I learned that recently."

It can get better. She longed for it to be. "Can I ask you a question?"

His head inched upward, apprehension on his face. "I suppose. You answered mine."

"Why haven't you married? You're successful, and you have a lovely home. You like animals, so I'm guessing you like kids. You have everything a woman could want."

Before finishing the question, she realized she'd struck a sour note with Martin. He'd flinched when she'd said he had everything a woman could want, and when she thought about her question, she cringed. "I'm not hinting about me, Martin. Please don't think I'm suggesting—"

His hand released hers, and he uncoiled their fingers. "Emily, I was married once."

She drew back, sensing the distance she'd created. How could she have been so stupid? "I'm sorry. I didn't know." She searched his face, witnessing the hurt in his eyes. "She died?"

He didn't respond, and Emily wanted to run into the house, but she was tired of running. Martin had offered her a friendship, and friends asked questions. Friends—

"She walked out on me."

Her hand flew to her mouth, her chest so tight she could barely breathe. "Martin, I had no idea. I shouldn't have asked."

"Why not? It's a natural question." His chin dropped to his chest. "It's one of those things I'm not proud of."

The pain in his eyes wound around Emily's heart. So that's why Steph told her Martin wasn't the marrying kind. He'd been hurt, too. In a different way than she had, but hurt was hurt. And he'd moved on with his life. "I can't imagine why a woman would leave you. I know you can be...abrupt."

"A jerk."

"Okay, you can be a jerk, but when two people love each other, they talk it out. Isn't that the way it's supposed to be? The Bible says if you have a grievance talk with the person who's upset you. Did she do that?"

"No, and I probably didn't either. Too much pride." He searched her face, then captured her hand in his. "But I don't grieve over her anymore, Emily. You know when Nick broke up with his fiancée years ago, I was actually happy because he'd failed, too. Can you believe it?"

She couldn't, but she understood.

"But that's long past, and I really think Denise leaving me was for the best. She wasn't happy, and I wasn't either, but I would have stuck it out. I'd made a vow to God."

Emily let his words weave through her mind. "Sometimes I think we do need too much, and we blame others for our own lack."

Martin squeezed her hand. "It's easy to blame everyone but ourselves. You're a smart lady."

"Sometimes." Her mind tangled around what he'd said. She'd spent her life blaming her parents for all the bad things they'd done. If she'd been smart, she would have wanted to be better than them, not the same. She would have tried to lift her life to another plane, not wallow in their poverty and immoral life. But she'd taken the easy road. She'd clung to the familiar, afraid to step outside the box. Times hadn't changed. The same fear held her back now...fear of taking a chance to change her life.

Martin released her hand. "Oops. If we're going to have dinner before seven, we'd better get back inside."

She pulled herself back to the present and rose from the chair, managing to focus on Martin as he beckoned her to follow.

He grasped the handle of the patio door. "Mom made a banana cream pie for dessert."

"She did?" His pleasure rippled through her.

"I think she's trying to beguile you." He chuckled.

"Beguile me for what?" The pleasant feeling tangled in her question.

"For her son."

*For her son.* The words roared in her mind. Could it be Julia was playing matchmaker? Concern and joy battled in her mind. Wisdom won out. She studied his half grin with a hint of question. "You're kidding?" She phrased her question with a hopeful ring that he was teasing.

His faint grin faded. "Being dead honest. Mother wants to see me married again."

Her stomach flipped, and she gasped for air. "How do you feel about that?" The look in his eyes fired her hopes and her apprehension.

"Time will tell."

*Time will tell.* She'd said the same thing to him about their friendship. The conversation left her confused. She wanted a better life, and she cared about Martin, but if she allowed herself to fall in love with him, she needed to be open. But she could never tell him everything he had a right to know. Never.

Martin lay in bed unable to sleep. The clock glowed on his nightstand, and he'd watched the minute hand inch its way past four o'clock with the speed of a snail. Too many things twisted in his mind. Telling Emily about his mother's matchmaking could be touted as his dumbest decision ever. He'd caught her off guard, and it wouldn't surprise him if she called in the morning and apologized her way out of going to church.

What had inspired him to tell her? He'd asked himself over and over since the confession had dropped from his mouth. He wanted to lift her spirits, he guessed. After her dire description of her childhood, she needed to know she had much to offer anyone, especially a man who found her attractive. He couldn't imagine living in a home that didn't acknowledge the day he was born. No matter how much jealousy he'd felt for Nick, his parents treated them the same when it came to birthdays.

But Emily had never experienced that. No birthdays. He ached for her. Maybe she'd been raised without family support or money, but somewhere along the line she'd learned compassion, and she'd learned strength. Even when she appeared uneasy as she'd cooked their meal, she didn't stop. She pushed herself forward and made the best out of a situation.

Thinking back, he realized he'd muddied her comfort level forcing her to cook, but the food had been delicious, and his mother had complimented her on the chicken. He'd even given her free rein with the rice pilaf once he explained what it was, and she'd added onions, mushrooms and even slivers of red pepper for color. He ended up sitting back while she made the salad, and then at the last minute, he decided to make a cheese sauce for the chicken.

Emily had done a wonderful job. Her vision hung in his mind. She'd stopped hiding behind those baggy clothes, and in his mind, the change reflected her new confidence as a woman. Maybe he was all wet. Perhaps the other outfits he'd seen had only been her work clothes. Whatever it was, he loved seeing her no matter what she wore.

His mother had witnessed the attraction in his eyes. He couldn't fool her. Ever. As a grown man, he had hoped he could hide a few simple things from his mother, but she did have that eagle eye that spotted everything. Nick could hide behind his smile and the twinkle in his eyes. Martin had decided long ago he'd missed the twinkle.

Rolling over, he grasped the pillow and buried his face in it. The clock's nagging gleam kept reminding him sleep had escaped him. He wondered if Emily ever lay in bed at night thinking of him. She'd endured so much in her life, and yet she seemed like a breath of fresh air. Although she struggled with her social naïveté, he found it charming. Something more had happened in her life though. He sensed it. He knew whatever it was, the mistake wasn't hers. She had a purity about her that set her above some of the women he knew. While he could see their manipulation, and their use of feminine wiles to get their way at his business and even in his few social circles, Emily exuded innocence. She didn't play games. What he saw was what he'd get with Emily. No pretenses.

He loved it. Love. The word fluttered through him. Attraction, yes. He realized he found her attractive in an amazing way. He enjoyed her company. Even missed her when she wasn't around. His fingers itched to call her on the phone, but he'd forced himself to take it easy. Too much could chase her away. She'd run off before. He didn't want it to happen again.

But love? He'd forgotten the feeling until now. Denise had sparked something in him. She'd been a user, but he had it to give, and she had social standing, things his father had always told him to look for in a prospective wife. His father's influence had been minimal, but when it came to business success, Martin had learned everything from his father.

With Emily it was different. She'd sparked something new and exciting in him. Her uniqueness had captured him. No games. No flirtation. No social climbing. Pure honesty to the point of being painfully honest. So why did he like that? Trust. He trusted her in some strange kind of way. Martin never knew what she might do. She'd hurried away from his house more than once, but she came back, and each time she brought with her greater strength. She'd changed. He hoped he'd done the same.

The blanket twisted around his waist, and he tossed it off while the clock shone the hour. Five a.m. He slipped his feet to the floor, tucked them into the moccasins he used as slippers and headed down the hall to the kitchen. He might as well enjoy a cup of coffee and maybe read his e-mail if he could concentrate. Martin headed for the coffeepot first, waited for the pot to start filling, then poured a cup and headed back to his computer.

He delved into e-mail, wrapped in the rich coffee aroma. When he finished, he opened a new document and jotted some notes to himself, wondering why he'd allowed his mind to settle into work issues on a Sunday morning. When he'd drained the last of his nearly cold coffee, Martin padded back to the kitchen and poured another cup. Surprised that more than an hour had passed, he settled into a chair, taking a sip of what he hoped might be enough caffeine to kick up his adrenaline. He had to get through a full day on little sleep.

The kitchen brought back memories of Emily tamping the chicken to flatten it, slicing the peppers and mushrooms, asking questions about cooking. He chuckled, thinking of Nessie following her from one location to the other, her eyes focused on whatever Emily had in her hand.

Finally, Nessie had found success, but it wasn't Emily who let the food drop, but he when he let a small slice of the chicken cordon bleu slip from the fork instead of reaching Emily's waiting mouth. He'd been eager for her to taste what she'd made. Nessie loved it. Emily did, too.

Martin lowered his head, the lack of sleep prodding

every nerve. He could easily play hooky from church, except his mother would have no part of it.

"Can't sleep?"

Her voice jolted him, and Martin glanced over his shoulder, seeing his mother dressed in a flowery robe standing in the kitchen doorway. "It happens sometimes."

A knowing look flickered on her face. "Problems?"

"No. Just random thoughts." He didn't look at her, certain the name Emily had become a neon light embedded in her forehead.

"Is it too early for breakfast?" She made her way to the refrigerator and looked inside. "Eggs and bacon. How's that sound?"

"Good, Mom, but you don't have to cook. I can do it."

"Too bad Emily's not here." She pulled out the items and set them on the counter before turning to him. "She did a lovely job with dinner."

He sat frozen, sensing his mother could actually read his thoughts. "Yes, she did."

He rose, thinking he would take over and avoid his mother's interrogation, but she was determined, so he sat back at the table while his mind conjured an escape. He could tell her he had to finish his e-mail, but he'd done all he cared to do.

Nessie stood by his feet looking at him, and he avoided the topic by letting her outside, then filled her dog food dish and water bowl.

"I'll get dressed, Mom. It won't take long."

She told him not to rush, and he hurried away, pleased with her suggestion. He'd definitely take his time. If he stuck around his mother too long, she'd have him spewing out every speck of emotion he'd tried to hide when it came to Emily. Emily had popped into his life only a month ago, and thoughts of marriage had already marched into his thoughts like a warrior ready to win a battle.

After showering, Martin slipped on his pants and shirt, eyed a tie and decided it would work with the sport coat he'd laid out. He grabbed his shoes and sank onto his bed, smelling the scent of bacon and eggs drifting in from the hallway. But instead of his mother, he pictured Emily in the kitchen. He bowed his head.

"Lord, is this Your plan? If it is, show me I am a husband worthy of a sweet woman like Emily."

The telephone's ring barraged his prayer. Martin rose and grasped the phone on his nightstand. He already knew it would be Emily saying she couldn't make it. His hello sounded feeble.

"I forgot to ask what time you'd pick me up for church."

Her voice sang in his ear, and Martin grinned at the phone, the sensation of well-being rippling through him. "About nine. Is that okay?"

"I'll be ready."

Could this be the Lord's way of answering his prayer?

"Did you sleep well?"

Air escaped him. "Not really."

"Me, neither."

He longed to ask why. "Too much rich food maybe."

"Maybe." Her breath rattled over the line. "I'll see you at nine."

He wanted to tell her how happy he was that she hadn't found an excuse not to go. Instead he said he'd see her soon and hung up.

"Lord, here I am. I want to be open and trusting. It's difficult. But I'm trying to be the man I can be. I've been so empty. I'm waiting for You to tell me what to do. All I can do is hope and pray."

Hope. It had been a long, long time since he'd really hoped.

# Chapter Nine

Music wrapped around Emily as she sat between Martin and Julia. The windows ahead of her opened to a lovely wooded setting, and the large floral display on each side of the Bible stand filled the backdrop with spring color. She drew in a lengthy breath, nudged by a sensation so different from feelings she'd experienced most of her life. Today she felt part of a family. The feeling warmed her, but again the old worry dampened her spirit.

Martin and Julia rose, and she joined them as the congregation sang a familiar hymn, one that took her back to the first days she'd learned that Jesus loved her despite all she'd done. At the end of the hymn, the pastor stood in the alcove while filtered sunlight dappled by leaf patterns splayed along the floor. Comfort settled over her. She glanced at Julia's rapt face, her eyes ahead tuned to the pastor's words.

Martin shifted beside her. She could feel his leg touching hers, and she drew in the scent of his aftershave. He looked handsome as always in dark pants and a beige sport coat. She'd never noticed the ring he wore on his right hand. She studied it, and when she drew her eyes away, she realized Martin had been watching her from the corner of his eye. Heat tinged her cheeks. She didn't want him to affect her as he did, but she couldn't will her feelings to stop. She'd tried.

The pastor's voice reached her with a message of hope. "The Bible reminds us it is not our ability alone that fulfills our dreams and purpose. It is the Lord's strength and promises that fires us with all we need for success and fulfillment. He gave us life and He promised to be with us and to guide us. Ephesians 3:20 says, *By His mighty power at work within us, He is able to accomplish infinitely more than we would dare to ask or hope.*"

The verse lodged in her mind. She'd tried to make her life better, but she had failed more than succeeded. Was she looking in the wrong place? Her mind soared with what lay within her grasp. God had opened windows and doors. She'd broadened her friendships. She'd found love in the animals and her new friends. Now, Martin and Julia had opened another door for her, but— She lowered her eyelids, feeling tears bead on her lashes. But the door could close. And worse, she could be the one who closed it.

Martin's hand touched hers. She controlled her emotions and looked at him, hoping the tears were hidden behind her eyes. He sent her a secret grin, slipped her hand in his and turned it over. She looked down and stiffened. The scar above her wrist, the jagged wound, glared at her.

She couldn't look at him, knowing what she might see written on his face. If he asked about the scars, she would tell him about her depression and her hopelessness. All she could do was pray he would understand.

The pastor's voice faded, and Martin turned her hand over again, hiding the scar. Air returned to her lungs. How long would she live with all of the baggage of her past hanging over her head like a hangman's noose?

When the service ended, Emily rose, her gaze averted from Martin's. They walked outside into the sunlight. Ahead in the curved driveway, she admired the large beds of flowers, purple, pink, yellow, and white blossoms with heads reaching upward to the sunlight.

She forced her chin up and gazed at Martin. "Thank you for inviting me. I loved the hymns."

Julia took her hand. "We loved having you." She gestured toward the colorful blooms. "Martin's going to take me to a nursery to pick up a few flowers. It's been so long since I've had my fingers in God's good earth."

"I told Martin he needs flowers in his yard." Emily reveled in the distraction.

"We could use another set of hands." Martin touched her shoulder. "I can stop by your place, and you can run in and change."

Her pulse tripped. "Would you mind, Julia?"

"Mind? I'd love the company." She tilted her head toward Martin. "You don't think he'll get his hands dirty, do you?"

Emily chuckled, willing the feeling to lift her spirit. "I'd love to help."

"As the pastor said in the sermon, this is more than I dared to ask or hope." He chuckled and slipped his arm around her shoulder, giving it a squeeze. "No time to lose while I have two willing workers."

The worry she'd had earlier dissipated in the anticipation of a visit to the nursery. Gardening certainly expressed hope. The farmer put seeds in the ground with expectation of growing food or flowers. Today, Emily would plant hope, too.

Martin leaned against the shovel and watched Emily work with his mother on the plants. Since he'd noticed the scar on her wrist he'd done everything to keep himself from asking her about it. His chest tightened each time the thought of her trying to take her own life. She couldn't have been that desperate, not the strong, amazing woman he'd gotten to know.

Other possibilities swept through his mind. Perhaps she put her hand through a jagged piece of glass. She may have fallen holding a bottle or glass plate. She may have— His jaw tightened. Emily had talked about her despondency years earlier, and he knew she hadn't been a believer back then.

He longed to hold her in his arms and tell her nothing could hurt her ever again, but saying that could be untrue. He'd fallen for her, but his confidence still wavered. Could he be a good husband? Relationships sparked trouble for him. He'd failed with Denise and even Suzette, and he'd only found success with Nessie because Emily had been at his side.

Enough. Emily wasn't Denise or a pet. She was a woman who deserved love and understanding. But he wasn't certain he could meet that need. He straightened and shifted the shovel. Stop asking for problems. Time will tell. They didn't need to rush.

Martin forced himself to focus on the flowers and the two women he cared about kneeling on the ground and digging their hands into the soil. His mother wore garden gloves, but Emily refused. "I like to feel the earth against my fingers," she'd said. "It's so real."

Reality. Emily appreciated truth and honesty. He'd told her nearly everything about his life and his flaws. He'd never done that before with a woman, and that's where he'd gone wrong.

"Good job, ladies." He drew back admiring the way they'd grouped the flowers by color, yellow in a cluster here and pink blossoms there.

"The ones in back are taller." Emily pointed to the purple flowers, their buds lifting above the green stems. "It'll be pretty when they fill out and spread."

He nodded, but his thoughts had left the flowers. Nothing was as lovely as Emily. "I'll trust you on that." He'd already made a point that he knew nothing about gardening. When he glanced at his mother, he noticed her stretch her back. She looked tired. He drew closer. "Mom, I'd like you to take a break. I don't want to send you home tonight exhausted or aching."

Emily nodded. "Julia, he's right. I can finish these." She grinned up at him. "And Martin will be happy to help, won't you?"

With a teasing frown, Martin rolled his eyes. "Definitely. I'd love to get my hands dirty."

His mother chuckled and shook her head. "You were never a good liar." She motioned to him. "Will you help me up?"

He laid down the shovel and helped her stand. Bracing her arm, he walked her inside to the recliner. "Let me get you something to drink."

"I'm fine." She settled into the chair, and Martin flipped up the footrest. "This is comfortable. I should buy one of these." She nestled her head against the cushion. "I might just take a little nap."

"Good idea." He watched her a minute until she closed her eyes, then slid open the patio screen door. "If you need me, yell. I can hear you, and I'll check on you in a minute."

She tilted her head upward and waved his words away. "I'm fine. Just tired. I'm not dying until the Lord wants me, and after that stroke, I think He still has something in mind for me down here."

Martin agreed and stepped outside. His mother wouldn't leave this earth until she knew both her sons were happy. She had one covered and one to go. The thought drew his attention back to Emily. He ambled to her side and crouched. "Okay, tell me what to do."

"I'm fine." She gazed at him, a smudge of dirt on her cheek.

He brushed it away, feeling the warmth of her skin in the afternoon sun. "I really want to help."

"I'll dig the holes, and you hand me the flowers."

That sounded easy, and he followed her direction until the rest of the plastic pots were empty. "Very nice." He stood and grasped her hand to hoist her up.

She stood a moment eyeing the flowerbeds. "It'll be beautiful in a couple of weeks. We just need to add a few things to the front."

"The front." He gave a slow nod. Emily would never give up. He slipped his arm around her waist. "Let's put these things back in the garage."

Emily gathered up the trowels, the small garden fork, and his mother's gloves. He tossed the last of the containers into the trash receptacle, then grasped the shovel and followed Emily around the house to the garage door. When she set the garden implements on a shelf, she brushed dirt from her hands, and Martin noticed the scar on her left hand.

Unable to pull his gaze away, Martin noticed her other wrist and caught his breath. Both had scars. His mind reeled as he turned away and swallowed bile that rose to his throat.

"Martin, what's wrong?"

His chest ached as he turned toward her, his eyes searching hers, wanting to know the answer, but he sensed she had no idea what had upset him. He swallowed again. Then without facing the repercussions, he lifted both of her hands in his and turned them over, revealing both scars.

Her face drained of color, and she lowered her lids. He felt her stiffen and sensed her desire to escape again, but he wouldn't let her if she tried.

She didn't try. She opened her eyes and drew in a ragged breath. "It was a long time ago before I knew the Lord. I had no hope. All I felt was self-pity and—"

Her face wrenched with pain. At that moment, Martin didn't care why it happened. He wanted to make it better. Feeling sorrow deeper than when Denise had walked out on him, he drew Emily into his arms. Her body quaked, and he braced her against him, holding her until she'd calmed.

When her eyes captured his, he lowered his lips to hers, the softness spiraling through his heart and into his quaking legs. He drew her closer, her mouth responding to his, and when he knew he had to stop, he eased back. His gaze swept over her lovely features, knowing that the greater beauty lie in her heart.

Martin wanted to tell her how he felt, to let her know the scars didn't affect his feelings, but no words could say what his heart felt. Instead he held her close again, their hearts beating in rhythm. His mind raced. Now that he'd kissed her, where would they go from here?

Emily shifted, and Martin loosened his hold. "I'm

sorry for all you've been through. My problems were nothing in comparison."

Her eyes searched his. "I could have told you about this, but—"

"Should haves and could haves aren't important. Today is important."

She blinked as if trying to grasp his meaning. But she understood what he meant. Today made all the difference in the world. This morning he'd heard what he needed to hear. He could accomplish more than he'd ever dared dream or ask. It only took time.

"Mike, can I talk with you a minute?" Martin stood in the doorway, eyeing his friend bent over his work.

"Sure." He lifted his head and beckoned him inside. As Martin approached, he rose and came around his desk. "Something wrong? I'm sure the report I gave you yesterday was—"

"It was fine. Excellent." He waved him back to his chair. "This is about me."

Mike sat and pointed to the chair in front of his desk, but Martin didn't sit. He ambled across the office, then spun on his heel and strode back. He finally focused on Mike, whose face looked as confused as Martin felt.

"That woman again?"

Martin's pulse skipped. "She's perfect...ly fine." He sank into the chair. "It's my head."

"Do I smell romance in the air?" Mike lifted his nose and sniffed. "I think I do."

Martin aimed a frown at him. "I need some fatherly advice, not that foolishness."

For his attempt at putting Mike in his place, all Martin received from him was a cocky grin. "Lay it on me."

"For an old man, you have an attitude." Martin recalled

his own and softened the frown. "Okay, here's how things are." He told Mike everything except about Emily's suicide attempt. With all that had happened, he needed to weigh his head and heart issues with someone he trusted.

Mike folded his hands on his desk and leaned across them. "You need a younger man than me to give advice, Martin. How about Nick?"

Martin had thought of Nick first. "My brother would tell his wife, and Steph would leak my concern to Emily. I don't need that in the mix. I'm confused enough."

"But you love her?"

The blunt question struck him between the eyes. "Love is something I haven't felt in years. I miss her when she's not around. I'm afraid of scaring her off. She's had a hard time in life, and my life may be too much for her, but I think if we give it time we could make it work."

"You think of her often?" Mike tapped his fingers on the desk.

"More than often. She's always in my thoughts."

Mike tilted his head. "Is it just, you know, pangs of—"

"Desire?" Martin shook his head. "I kissed her and enjoyed every second of it, but I stopped. I respect her, and she's too good to be taken advantage of. I see her sitting beside me in the family room with a fire in the grate. Sitting with me in church. Walking with me in the park...with Nessie, of course." He dragged lightheartedness from his whirring thoughts.

Mike held up his hand like a cop. "You can stop. I get the picture. It's serious, Martin. Don't doubt it. So if that's the case, what can't you decide?"

"How to proceed. She's backed away each time

I've stepped too close, except the kiss, and then she was—"

"If the lady didn't run from that, she's probably dealing with the same things you are. Stop worrying. Get old-fashioned. It worked years ago. Why not now?"

"Old-fashioned?" He pictured horse and buggies and ice cream socials.

"Court her. Woo her. Easy does it. Surprise her with something special. What does she like?"

"Dogs."

Mike tapped his finger against his head. "Think. Yes, dogs, but what else. Special things."

"Flowers. She loves them." His chest tightened. "She's never had a birthday celebration. No party. Nothing. Not even cupcakes." His pulse accelerated. She deserved a bakery. "I'll do something special for her birthday. That's a start, isn't it."

Mike rose and slipped his hands into his pant pockets. "See. You didn't need me at all. A birthday celebration. Invite her friends and family."

"That's the problem. No family." He eyed Mike. "I realize you don't know her, but how about rounding out the table. Mom will be alone."

"Julia? I'd love to, and I'd like to meet this young woman that's on your mind."

Young woman. She was, but he hoped that didn't matter. "Great. It's the twenty-second of this month. Saturday. Hold the evening."

Mike chuckled. "I wish all your problems were this easy to resolve."

Martin shook his head. Nothing had been resolved, but he had been motivated. He glanced over his shoulder at Mike and gave him a thumbs-up, relieved he had a plan. He drew up his shoulders. He'd invite Emily's coworkers and their husbands, his mother and Mike. Now to do it right and make it memorable for Emily.

## Chapter Ten

Emily refilled the last of the dogs' water containers and walked into the office. She checked the wall clock, and it matched her watch. For some reason today, she'd felt antsy. She loved her time at the shelter. It gave her purpose and the dogs gave her love, but today she felt different.

The jingle of the telephone caused her to jump, but at least the sound was something to break up the day. "Yes, we have a five-year-old setter and a pointer puppy. We're open until eight tonight."

The door tinkled, and a young man stepped inside carrying a white box. She held up her finger. "Wonderful. We'll see you around seven then." She loved watching families pick up a new dog, but not enough to stay late. Dee would be in to take over.

She turned to the young man. "May I help you?"

"Will you sign for this box?" He shoved a paper in front of her.

She eyed the cardboard container. "What is it?"

He shrugged. "I was paid to deliver it. I don't pack the

boxes." He tapped the bill with his index finger. "Sign here."

Her focus settled on the box logo. Give Thanks Bakery? Confused, she picked up a pen. "I'm not sure this is the right address. I didn't—"

"Time for Paws on Rochester." He gazed around the room. "Looks right to me."

She shrugged and signed her name, figuring Steph must have ordered something. She watched him tear off a copy of the form, place it on the box top and walk out. Curious, Emily picked up the phone and hit the buzzer.

One buzz, and Steph answered. "What's up?"

Emily studied the package. "Did you order something from Give Thanks Bakery?"

"Not me. What is it?"

"I don't know. A box."

She hung up and stared at the bakery's logo, but before she could open it, Steph came through the doorway. "Is it ticking?"

Emily shook her head. "Funny."

"Well, open it. If it's something from the bakery, this baby is excited." She gave her belly a pat.

String held down the lid, and Emily reached into the draw for scissors and snipped it off. She lifted the lid and dropped it back. "Cupcakes." She eyed Steph. "Is this a joke?"

"A joke? Not from me." She dipped her finger into the dark coating of chocolate and licked it. "What's funny about cupcakes?"

Emily faltered, struck by the significance. She eyed the calendar. Who knew? Tears bubbled in her eyes, and she tried to swipe them away before Steph noticed. "Today's my birthday."

"Really?" She lifted the cupcake she'd fingered. "You don't mind, do you?"

Emily managed a grin. "Not at all. Have two." Martin's face filled her mind. He was the only one she'd ever told about the cupcakes.

Steph lowered the treat and eyed her. "Emily." She set the treat back into the box and wrapped her arms around Emily's shoulders. "You really were surprised."

Along with her ragged breath, she managed to get out a yes.

"Who sent this? Martin?"

She drew back, releasing a pent up breath. "I imagine. No one else knew, I think."

"You see. He can be a good guy after all. I told you not to worry about working with him."

Emily longed to tell her it was more than that, but if she spoke the words they would become too real. Martin's actions today touched her more than she could have imagined. Her hand trembled as she studied the contents of the box. She chose a pastry that had a dark chocolate crust. When she bit in, a rich cream gushed through the chocolate followed by a moist devil's food cake. She licked her fingers. "This is so good."

"And you can afford to put a little meat on those bones." Steph gave her another hug. "Do you have birthday plans tonight?"

When did she ever have plans other than walking dogs? "I'm not one for celebrations."

"If I didn't have plans, I'd suggest we go out to dinner or something."

Emily's heart twisted. "The thought is more than enough."

The door tinkled again, and Dee swung into the office, eyeing the box. "What's that?"

Emily explained and offered her a cupcake.

Dee dropped her handbag and delved into the box. "Happy birthday, Emily. If we'd known, we could have decorated the office or something." When she lifted the cupcake, she reached in with the other hand and pulled out a small envelope. "You missed this."

Emily peered at it, an edgy feeling creeping up her back.

"Take it, Emily." Steph gave her an elbow poke. "It's not a singing telegram. You have to read it."

Steph's usual humor pushed Emily forward. She took the paper from Dee and opened it. The words swam in her eyes. *I would love to have you join me for dinner tonight. I'll pick you up at seven. Martin.* Emily's heart beat so hard she feared she couldn't speak.

"Martin?" Steph's question marched into the air.

She nodded and slipped the note back into the envelope. "He invited me to dinner."

"Good for him." Steph wrapped her arm around her shoulder. "Now, you have plans."

Dee licked her fingers and grabbed another cupcake. "Girl, you can leave a little early on your birthday, especially since you have a date."

"I don't have to leave early, and it's not a date. It's—"

Both women snickered and looked at her as if she'd lost her mind.

She ignored their reaction and suggested they keep the treats at the shelter, but they wouldn't hear of that either. Dee flapped the box closed while Steph draped Emily's shoulder bag over her arm and plopped the package into her hand. They stood at the door and shooed her off. She felt like a chicken who wanted to sit on her nest while they chased her through the doorway to face the fox. She pictured Martin's handsome face. Fox fit him well.

Emily stared in her closet for fifteen minutes, pairing skirts with blouses, then pulled out her one dress and worried it wasn't nice enough. She'd worn it to Steph's wedding, but she'd dressed it up with the yellow jacket. She had no idea if the restaurant was plain or fancy. She plopped on her futon and stared at her clothes lined up in the small closet. Her mind slipped back to Martin's closet. He had room to spare. But then so did she since she had so few clothes, especially ones that needed hanging.

She'd managed. She didn't need dressy clothes when she walked dogs. Pants and tops fit her lifestyle. They didn't fit Martin's. Ignoring her negative comment, she rose and trudged across the room. With determination, she flipped open the bakery box and grabbed another of the chocolate dipped cakes. The filling oozed out and soothed her until she looked at the clock. Only twenty-five minutes to get ready.

The dress seemed her only choice. She pulled it from the hanger and tossed it on the futon, then opened a drawer and nosed inside, hoping to find something to dress it up. The beige dress could look fine with most anything, but that's what she didn't have.

The clock hands jerked upward, and she stood at the bathroom mirror, reapplying her makeup she'd washed off in the shower. She ran a brush through her hair swept it back, letting it fall in waves to her shoulders. At least she had some natural curl going for her. She eyed the beige color against her pale skin. She felt drab.

Her mind sparked an idea. She dug into a lower drawer searching for a silk scarf she used in winter. It was light weight with beige background and hues the color of a peacock. That would brighten up the dress. When she saw the flash of turquoise, she grasped the long scarf and pulled it out. A Caribbean sea. That was the color—beige sand mingled with the multi-hued water. One day she'd see it for real. She pictured herself lolling on a beach, watching water lapping to the shore. Photographs weren't enough, anymore.

Wrinkles creased the silk fabric, and she pulled out the iron and plugged it in, then looked in her jewelry box for a brooch or pin. An amber-looking stone sat in a gold-plated setting, and she pulled it out. She had no idea where it came from, but it would work. Emily steamed the scarf, turned off the iron, and headed back to the mirror. In a few moments, she'd draped the scarf around her neckline and attached it on one side, letting one end flow over her shoulder and the shorter end, she clasped with the pin and fanned out the silk. It worked.

If she'd known a birthday dinner would cause so much stress, Emily would have declined, but Martin's kindness washed away the frustration of her limited wardrobe. He'd become a true friend, more caring and thoughtful than her own parents had been. She pictured them nearly comatose with alcohol, and she guessed drugs too. They had been flower children in their day, and they had never become fully-fledged adults. She and her sister had suffered the consequences. And her parents had faced theirs. They'd died too young.

In contrast, Julia came to mind. Maybe she hadn't done everything right, but she'd raised two successful sons. She could be proud of that no matter what flaws she thought she had. They'd been believers, too, and the Lord had His way when He had a plan.

Emily wondered if God had a plan for her.

A noise caused her to falter, and she realized it was a knock. She gave another glance in the mirror, drew in a breath, and opened the door.

Martin stood in the hallway holding a bouquet of flowers. "Happy birthday." He held them out to her, and she did all she could not to let her emotion carry her away.

"You've already done so much, Martin. You didn't have to—"

"Hush. This is your birthday. You can't begrudge a friend from enjoying your day with you."

Embarrassed she hadn't accepted the flowers graciously, she thanked him, then backed up and stared into her small kitchenette. She didn't have a vase so no sense looking, and she couldn't just toss them on the counter. She focused. A pitcher. She had that. In moments, she'd clipped the flower stems and arranged them. "What do you think?" She turned to show him.

"Beautiful."

His eyes said it all as he gazed at her and not the bouquet. Frazzled, she turned back and set them on her small table. "Thank you, Martin. They're lovely."

He took her hands, stood back, gazing at her again from head to toe. "You're lovely, Emily. You look radiant." He drew her into his arms.

"Because I'm blushing."

He leaned back, his serious look brightened by a chuckle. She noticed the flash of dimple on his cheek. He gave her a squeeze and released her. "Are you ready?"

She nodded and grasped her handbag, her heart pounding with anticipation of their evening together.

They headed down Main Street into downtown Rochester. Martin pulled into a parking area and jumped out. She waited, aware that he always tried to open the door for her, but she always beat him to it. This time he opened it and watched as she slipped out. He took her hand and led her toward the neon marquee, its lights announcing Andiamo Osteria. Martin approached the glass and chrome door and pulled it open.

Inside, rich aromas drifted from the dining area, whose decor contained light-toned wood and real tablecloths and red cloth napkins. Vines and plants twisted along a bamboo-like wall dividing two dining areas on different levels. The elegance overwhelmed her, and she feared she might embarrass Martin, not knowing which knife or fork to use.

Martin guided her as they followed the maître d' toward the back of the restaurant, and when they neared their table, Emily's heart rose to her throat. She gazed at Molly and Brent, then Steph and Nick and finally Julia and a man she didn't know. She grasped Martin's arm. "What is this?"

"A birthday party."

Her pulse skipped as tears blurred her eyes. A party. She shook her head, remembering she'd confessed she'd never had a party. Martin squeezed her hand as she brushed away the tears.

Trying to overcome her emotions, Emily watched as everyone rose and approached her. Her heart thudded as she hugged her friends. Julia stepped close and wrapped her arms around her as she whispered happy birthday in Emily's ear.

Flabbergasted, Emily found no words to respond to the amazing surprise. She gazed at them, one at a time, thinking of the planning and the secret they'd kept from her.

"You knew," she said to Steph, who watched her with a conspiring grin.

"Did you want me to spoil the surprise?"

She didn't need to answer the question. Words finally found her. "This is one of the best days of my life. Thank you so much. I'm—" She covered her eyes, struggling to gain control of her emotions, but she lost the battle as tears rolled down her cheeks. Courage rose inside her as she decided to be open. "I've never had a birthday party before."

Steph came to her rescue. "And nothing could top this."

Emily managed to smile as Martin's arm tightened around her shoulder. He introduced her to his friend, Mike Schumer, and Emily noticed that he and Julia seemed to be friends. The waiter arrived and took their drink orders as she perused the menu. The prices startled her, and unable to avoid looking at them, she folded the menu and caught Martin's attention. "Would you choose something for me?"

A faint scowl flashed before it faded. "With your approval."

She agreed, and in minutes, he leaned closer. "I hope you like Italian."

"I love it."

When the waiter returned, he ordered veal scaloppini for her and a homemade pasta dish for him. While the others ordered, Emily admired the surroundings and listened to the music drifting to the tables. The hum of voices and the candles glinting in the glass globes around the room mesmerized her.

The drinks arrived, drawing her back to the party, and when she looked up, wrapped packages had appeared on the table. Her throat constricted. Cupcakes, flowers, dinner and now gifts. Martin had planned a celebration woven with everything any child or adult could want for a birthday. He'd grown more wonderful every day, and even his do-me-a-favor mode had lightened.

The fragrance of coffee drifted past her. She lifted her water glass embellished with a slice of lemon and took a sip to wet her dry mouth.

Martin pushed the gifts closer to her. "Why not open your presents before we eat."

She eyed the packages, then gazed at their smiling faces. "Thank you all. This is very special to me."

"Open mine and Molly's." Steph slipped a gift bag toward her.

Inching out the tissue, she withdrew a small envelope, and deeper inside, she found a colorful silk scarf. It would have been an answer to her quandary earlier when she searched for something to wear. The shades of blue had streaks of golden thread that glittered in the candlelight. "It's beautiful." The soft fabric slithered across her fingers, and her chest burst with their thoughtfulness.

"Open the card." Molly grinned, wagging her finger at the envelope.

She pulled it open and chuckled at the message, but when she glanced down, a gift certificate had fallen to the table. "Molly. Steph. This is— I—"

"It's from all of us." Nick's voice cut through her hesitation. She eyed the gift amount and shook her head. "Thank you so much."

They applauded, and Julia pointed to another gift bag. Inside she found a cross on a gold chain. She'd never owned a cross and the thoughtful gift touched her. She lifted her gaze to Julia, forcing herself not to say anything but thank you.

"It's old, Emily. I have two crosses, and I can only wear one so I wanted to give it to you with wishes for many years of blessings."

"It's lovely. I'll cherish it." She leaned over and kissed Julia's cheek. When she looked at her, Julia's eyes were glazed with tears.

The waiter arrived, interrupting the moment, and they quieted as they delved into their salads. Conversation drifted to many things from birthdays to the shelter to the men's businesses, and near the end of the meal, Martin slipped his hand into hers beneath the table and gave it a squeeze.

When the meal ended, Emily drew in a lengthy breath, still amazed at the lavish celebration. "I couldn't eat another bite."

A chuckle rippled over the group, and she followed their gazes and looked over her shoulder. The waiter stood behind her with a birthday cake, its candles lit. She made a wish at their insistence, but the wish was more a prayer. "My thirty-third birthday will go down in history as the best birthday ever." When she'd finished, they broke into the happy birthday song. In the flurry of their singing, the waiter had taken away the cake, and now returned with it sliced into eight pieces, then boxed the rest. Cupcakes and cake. Time for Paws would have treats when she arrived at work on Monday.

Coffee was poured as she forced a few bites of the delicious cake, and though they all chattered about many things, Martin seemed quieter, but no one seemed to notice except her.

After coffee refills, Martin pushed away his plate and cup and flagged the waiter. He slipped him a credit card, and when the bill had been settled, she gathered her gift bags while Martin carried the leftover cake. Outside, goodbyes were said, and Emily slipped into Martin's car, trying to decide what had quieted him.

Martin shifted into Reverse and pulled onto Main

Street, heading toward her apartment. When he rolled into her parking lot, she reached for the handle, but Martin grasped her other hand. "Emily."

She faltered and turned back to face him.

"Do you realize I'm ten years older than you?"

She studied his expression. His face appeared etched with concern. "I knew you were older than me."

"You did?"

"Nick is forty-one, I think, and you're his older brother. It seemed logical." She searched his face to make sense out of his concern.

"You don't care?"

"Care? Why should I? No one said friends have to be the same age." She shifted to face him. "I love your mom. I consider her a friend, and—"

His cell phone jarred her.

His expression didn't change.

Tension knotted her neck. "Aren't you going to answer it?"

"No. I'm sure it's nothing."

"I don't agree. We've been with your family all evening, who else would be calling you this late?" She grasped the door handle again, but he held up his index finger as he fumbled for his phone.

The ringing stopped.

She watched his expression as he eyed the missed call.

He lifted his gaze from the phone. "It was Nick."

"Call him back. It must be important." Her hand remained on the door handle, but couldn't convince herself to open the door.

He looked at her a moment before hitting the call button.

"Nick?" A frown grew on his face as he listened.

When he glanced her way, his eyes told her something was wrong. Julia. Tension rolled down her back.

"Which hospital?" He looked at Emily again. "I'll be there in a few minutes." He flipped the phone closed.

Tension knotted her. "Your mother?"

"No. It's Steph."

Her heart thundered. "The baby? It's too early."

"I know, but she's having contractions."

Emily sat frozen, unable to move, her prayers flying to Heaven.

"Do you want to go with me?"

His voice wrapped around her. "Yes, if you don't mind."

He shifted into gear and pulled away.

# Chapter Eleven

Martin's head pounded as he headed into Crittenton Hospital emergency. The dark night wrapped around him in silence. Emily walked beside him, staring straight ahead, tears pooling on her lashes. He'd sent up prayer after prayer since Nick's call, and he realized how unimportant his concerns were about Emily's age and every other issue he'd created to mess up his head.

The security guard spoke to them before allowing them inside. The sliding door opened, and Martin held back, allowing Emily to enter first. A woman at the desk guided them to the emergency waiting room, but when they entered, Nick wasn't there. Emily headed for a chair, and he followed, his nerves in knots.

He sat beside her. In his peripheral vision, he saw Emily brush tears from her eyes. He longed to hold her in his arms and ease the tension knitting her jaw. When Nick called with the news, he realized what love meant and how it felt. He heard fear in Nick's voice and his love for Steph powered Nick's optimism. Tonight Martin longed to have Emily love him. Hope for the future had rarely been part of his thoughts, but when it came to Emily, it seemed to be all he had on his mind. But tonight his hope belonged to Nick, Steph and the baby who needed a few more weeks before making an appearance.

"Do you know anything about early birth?" His voice sounded loud in the stillness of the room.

Emily's head jerked upward, and her expression appeared as stressed as his own. "Premature birth? Not really."

"What happens if Steph gives birth now? I mean... will the baby—"

"She's due next month. We need to pray. That's all I know." Worry snapped in her voice.

"I've been doing that since Nick's call."

Emily shifted, her voice more encouraging. "Maybe it's false labor. If not, they have medication to stop it, I think." She shook her head as her optimism flagged. "I hope."

He slipped his hand over hers as if his touch could make everything better. Emily cared as much as he did about Steph and the baby. Sometimes friendships were stronger than even family.

Her family came to mind. He'd experienced a good life in comparison. He'd created many of his own problems growing up and had spent a lifetime blaming his parents. Now his vision had cleared. Yes, they had expectations, but it was because they loved him and wanted him to be successful. And he had been.

A movement at the doorway captured his attention, and he glanced up, but it wasn't Nick or anyone he knew. The birthday dinner seemed ages ago instead of just hours. On the way to the hospital as he passed Andiamos again, he envisioned the wonderful evening. Emily's surprised expression still glowed in his mind. "Did you think Steph seemed different tonight?"

Emily drew in a breath and gazed at him. "She seemed quieter near the end of dinner."

"That's what I was thinking. She usually tosses in a few sharp-witted comments in the course of a conversation, but I don't remember her saying much of anything."

Emily shook her head. "She must have been having some symptoms then."

Symptoms. He and Emily had symptoms that had lasted a lifetime. Tonight their problems seemed inconsequential. Emily had talked about friendship not having age barriers, and that was his problem. Friendship didn't matter when it came to age, but he feared it could be a problem for two people in a committed relationship.

Committed relationship? Why couldn't he say the word? Marriage. His pulse skipped with the admission. Most men wanted to be a protector and provider for their families. Emily needed both, and he could give her anything she needed. Everything she longed for. If only—

"Martin."

His head jerked upward when he heard Nick's voice. He rose and opened his arms. Nick settled into his embrace. "How is she? What's happening?"

"They're trying to hold off labor." Nick drew back, recognition registering on his face. "Emily. Thanks for coming. I—"

"I'd be miserable at home, Nick."

He stepped beside Emily and gave her a quick hug. "They're checking her again. It's only the thirty-sixth week, and—"

"The baby needs forty." Emily murmured the comment almost to herself.

"As close as possible." Nick stared into space a moment.

Martin put his arm around his shoulder. "You look exhausted."

"I am." Nick rubbed his hand over his face. "I think I'll sit for a while. They'll let me know when I can see her again."

He sat and Martin settled between him and Emily. Silence settled over them, and his mind snapped into a place he hadn't wanted it to go. Nick would become a father. He would have a child who was part of him, one that would carry on when he was gone. Emptiness shivered in Martin's heart. A child of his own. A child to raise with wisdom. Cheering the child's successes and accepting his son's weaknesses. If he'd learned nothing from his past, Martin longed to be a good father, providing his son with strength and confidence.

But could that happen? He gazed at Emily. Was she the woman who could overlook his shortcomings and embrace the few good qualities he had? He longed for God to give him a sign and to offer him assurance. Being hurt again would be his undoing. Trust and faith. He needed both.

Emily's arm shifted against his. The soft touch stimulated his longing yet triggered a warning. She leaned across him toward Nick. "When did Steph start having problems?"

Nick filled them in with her first twinges of pain at the restaurant and then the stronger pains after they'd left. "We came straight here after we dropped off Mom." He lowered his head and rubbed his face in his hands. "You know Steph. She didn't want to worry her."

"You mean Mom doesn't know." Martin twinged with concern. "She'll be upset if she's left out of the loop."

Nick drew in a lengthy breath. "I'll call her once I know something. Why stress her now?"

Martin nodded, realizing he was right.

Nick straightened his back. "I couldn't believe Steph. Rather than worry about herself, she spent the trip here wondering what she'll do about the shelter. She hasn't found anyone yet to fill in next month, let alone now."

Emily slid to the edge of her chair. "Nick, I'll be happy to help. I can fit in the dog-walking somehow, and I can fill for Steph part-time. She has Dee working part-time too, so maybe between the two of us, we can pick up the slack. And Dee might be able to add some hours. I'll ask her for you."

"Will you? That would be great and it will stop Steph's fretting."

Martin kept his mouth shut but didn't like what he heard. If Emily put in more hours at the shelter and squeezed in her dog-walking, when would he see her?

"Mr. Davis."

Martin's head snapped upward. Nick rose and headed for the doorway. Martin forced himself to lean back in the chair and wait for Nick to return. Emily had shifted back in the seat, too, her back rigid, her focus glued to the doorway.

He took advantage of Nick's absence. "Taking over Steph's doggie day care is a huge job. Do you know what you've committed yourself to?"

She eyed him. "I can't sit here and not offer to help. I can't do everything, but I can pitch in. We all will, and if—" she nodded her head toward the door "—if things get worse, then Molly can hire someone for Steph. Molly would do that." She shook her head. "It's not about convenience, Martin. We've talked about that. It has to do with helping a friend. Giving, not taking."

Her sharp words penetrated his heart. He'd admitted being a person who did things when it was convenient, and he'd tried to make amends, but—

"I'm sorry." Emily touched his arm. "I didn't mean to attack you. You've been so wonderful to me. Tonight was amazing. The whole day has been unbelievable, and I—"

Tears flooded her eyes, and Martin slipped his arm around her shoulder, sad he'd made her cry. "We're both upset." He moved his hand against her soft arm, longing to hold her closer. "Let's see what Nick says. Hopefully it will be good news."

Emily rested her head on his shoulder, and in moments, her breathing told him she'd fallen asleep. He gazed at her innocent face. Despite her difficult years, she'd escaped the callousness that sometimes happened to people who'd stopped feeling. The tears in her eyes validated the amount of love Emily had for others. Sometimes he still could hide behind a stoic expression, but since he'd gotten to know Emily, hiding his feelings had become difficult.

The wall clock hands crept from number to number, and when Nick returned, his face had darkened with worry. Martin wakened Emily and rose. "How's it going?"

As if trying to get his emotions in check, Nick paused before he spoke. "She's having regular contractions, and the doctor said it's almost hopeless to try and stop them now."

"Steph's in real labor?" Emily's voice hitched.

Nick drew up his shoulders. "I'd hoped this wouldn't happen, but—" He covered his face with his hands.

Helplessness washed over Martin. He'd never seen his brother cry, and at the moment, his own grief had tightened his vocal chords. "They'll be fine, Nick." The words choked from his throat. "Steph's strong, and knowing that about both of you, the baby will come out fighting."

With his head still lowered, Nick pulled his hands away and brushed his eyes. "Where's my faith?"

"It's right where you left it, Nick." He placed his hand over Nick's heart. "Your faith is strong. Never doubt it. We're all praying, and we'll be here with you." He grasped his brother's arm and gave it a shake. "I'm not going anywhere."

Emily stood beside Nick gazing at the tiny child enclosed in a plastic basinet that would keep the little girl's body temperature normal. The nurse explained that the sensors taped to the baby monitored her blood pressure, heart rate, breathing and temperature. Too much for Emily to comprehend as she gazed at the infant and then at Nick standing beside her.

The nurse gave them a faint smile. "I know this seems dire, but truly, your little girl is strong and her weight is better than many. She's five pounds and that's good news."

Five pounds. A sack of flour or sugar. Emily couldn't comprehend how this tiny being would become a woman one day.

Nick's tensed body shuddered, and Emily slipped her arm around his back. "It is good news."

"Steph isn't in danger. I'm grateful for that."

His tone had a bite to it, as if his faith had flagged. She longed to remind him that with God all things were possible. Everything happened for the good of those who loved Him.

"Do you have a name for her?"

"A name?" He gave her a blank look.

"Your daughter. Did you pick out a name?"

Nick's face brightened. "We'd talked about Mackenzie or Megan. Julia will be her middle name."

She patted his back. "Your mom will love that."

"Speaking of Mom, did Martin leave to pick her up yet?" He glanced over his shoulder toward the doorway.

"He left after he walked me here." She eyed her watch. "They should be here in another fifteen or twenty minutes." She dropped her arm. "I think I'll go back to the waiting room now so you can sit with Steph."

His eyes averted, Nick nodded, looking down at the floor. He tucked his hands in his pockets and they retreated to the doorway.

"I can find my way back. You go ahead."

Zombie-like, he turned and walked away while Emily stood a moment, wondering about the tiny life in jeopardy except for God's mercy. A prayer flooded her mind as she made her way back to the waiting room. She poured a cup of strong coffee and settled into the chair she'd been in for hours, realizing she would have to go to work without sleep. Sometimes she had Sunday off, but not this Sunday.

Midnight had long passed and so had her birthday. Martin's surprise washed over her. He'd done everything anyone could do to make up for the lack of celebration she'd experienced over the years. Like a dream, the day seemed unreal, too wonderful to be reality. But it had been. Martin gave her a new reality every day. Longing crept through her, the desire to be a mother and wife, but she didn't know how.

Martin seemed on his best behavior lately, almost too perfect as if he'd taken lessons in being a thoughtful man who cared about her. When she remembered his inability to handle Suzette and then his problems with Nessie, she wondered how he'd learned the skill of impressing a woman so quickly. She chuckled. The emotion released the tension from her body, and determination took its place. If God listened to prayer and answered it, then she would pray. Not for herself today, but for Steph and Nick and the tiny little girl in the incubator ready to meet the world with loving parents.

Loving parents. Would she ever have the chance to be a mother? Being a parent had always been inconceivable, not even a vague possibility. A sliver of envy snaked through her, a desire she'd never felt before. Envy. She loathed the feeling. How did Martin feel, witnessing his youngest brother's beautiful offspring? He hadn't said much, but his eyes had spoken his concern for the baby. She squirmed against the chair longing for sleep but wanting to stay alert.

A magazine caught her attention, and Emily grasped it and flipped open the pages. The words blurred, and she closed her eyelids for a moment.

"Emily."

She snapped open her eyes and looked into Martin's blurred face. Awareness slipped into her consciousness.

"You were sleeping."

Emily blinked, realizing she had been. The magazine had slipped between her and the chair arm. Her gaze searched behind him. "Where's your mother?"

"With Nick." He lowered himself into the chair beside

her, looking as exhausted as she felt. "She's doing fine. Totally confident that the baby will breeze through this."

"I think so, too. Steph and Nick will make great parents. God knows their need."

She tried to pull herself together. Her eyes felt heavy, and she sensed her makeup had faded except for her mascara, which she fully expected to be black smudges beneath her eyes.

Martin rested his palm against her arm. "You have to work today, right?"

She nodded, questioning her good sense but having little choice. "I need to be there."

"Mom will stay with Nick while I drive you home."

The touch of his hand spread a comforting warmth through her. She gazed into his eyes, aware of how much he meant to her. How much his family meant. The feeling raced to her heart and sent chills down her arms. One day she hoped her amazing feelings wouldn't be followed by the iciness of disappointment.

Though she didn't want to go, she realized Martin was right. She would be more useful at the shelter, and Steph would rest better, knowing her doggie day care was in good hands. Inside Martin's car, she leaned her head against the headrest and closed her eyes, but when they reached Rochester Road, Martin's voice roused her.

As if he hadn't noticed, Martin began talking about his mother—how excited she was and how she was confident everything would be fine. But Emily sensed something else in Martin's voice, and she wished he'd tell her what it was.

He didn't. His avoidance poked at her until she couldn't stop herself. "What are you thinking?"

He glanced her way, confusion written on his face. "You mean about the baby?"

"Not necessarily. I sense something else is on your mind."

He drew in a breath. "Am I that obvious?"

"You look more thoughtful than concerned. That's why I asked."

He didn't respond until he'd turned off the radio station, faintly audible against the usual traffic noises. "I'm thinking of my mom. She's a new grandmother, and her excitement caught me unaware. I don't know why, but it did. And I'm an uncle. I suppose it sounds silly, but it's made me connect with my family in a different way, a positive way, and..."

"Martin, those are good feelings. Family connections makes a person complete, I think."

He gave her thoughtful look, as if he understood that she'd never had the experience.

"I feel the same in a strange sort of way. I'm not family but yours has opened the door to me to share part of what you have. It's good to feel connected."

"I don't agree with you, though, on one thing." His voice had grown thoughtful.

She waited.

"I'm not sure it's family that makes a person complete. It's more than that."

The idea slithered down her back. "In what way?"

"I'm not really complete even with a close relationship with my mom and Nick. Even though I'm part of a larger family unit, I don't have a family of my own."

*Family of my own.* His yearning pierced her heart. She understood all too well.

"Complete to me means a wife with God's blessing, and if He wills, children. Now that's complete."

He flashed a questioning look her way, then turned his attention to the highway.

Emily sank deeper into the cushion, her thoughts swirling around what he'd said.

The morning sun charged across the horizon. Her eyes stung with the glare, and she closed them, with questions fading into the tug of sleep.

# Chapter Twelve

Martin lifted the box from his car and headed for the doggie day care in the rear of Time for Paws. The scent of food drifted up, causing his stomach to roll with the stimulus. He'd wrapped the casserole in towels to keep it warn. He hadn't seen Emily except for brief encounters. She'd become a shadow, there and gone when he turned away. He'd stopped by the shelter a couple of times to see her, and once when she had visited Steph, he'd stopped by. Everyone worked to encourage Steph while she waited for Megan to be released from the hospital. The baby had improved so much that her coming home looked promising.

Using one hand to balance the box, Martin opened the day care door and stepped inside, greeted by Emily's surprised expression.

"What are you doing here?" The surprise faded as she eyed the box. She sniffed the air as her expression changed to appreciation. "You brought me food?"

"Homemade, and it's for both of us."

She gave him a dubious look as she scanned the office. "You plan to eat on this desk?"

"I could, but I brought along a card table." He held up a finger. "I'll get it." Before she could say anything else, he hurried outside and pulled the table from the trunk. He'd come prepared for her to say he shouldn't have bothered. He'd become accustomed to that, but he was unwilling to accept her refusal. She'd been eating sandwiches and soup she'd heated in the microwave. The last time he'd seen her she looked gaunt. Even her new clothes hung on her. Someone had to take care of her, even if she didn't take care of herself.

Emily stood in the center of the room along with her desk chair and another small chair she had there for clients. She had the same questioning look on her face.

He snapped open the table legs, trying to understand why Emily didn't catch on to his ulterior motive. Maybe she'd never heard the old-fashioned word "courting." No one used the term anymore except someone like Mike, but Martin knew the concept, and he was giving it his all. With other attempts, all he'd done was chase her away. Courting her needed subtlety, and that's what he was trying to accomplish.

Though courting was purposeful, he still had a difficult time getting a grip on his emotions. He'd allowed his heart to take over his common sense. Even if Emily recognized his desire for a committed relationship, could she love him? And why did he assume he was lovable? Reassurance would help, but he couldn't ask Steph or Molly what they thought. His brother would think he was nuts if he posed the question to him, and yes, his mother would agree he was lovable, because she looked at him with a mother's eye.

Emily had finally dug inside the box containing his dinner surprise. "You brought a tablecloth."

Martin took it from her hand and flung it over the card

table, realizing too late it was one of his large ones. He pulled it off and folded it in half. Though still too long, it no longer piled on the floor.

Carrying two plates, Emily headed for the table and set them down, her eyes asking questions. She'd experienced so little in her life that someone bringing her a meal must have seemed unbelievable to her.

He ignored the look and unwrapped the casserole of pasta and chicken drenched in tomatoes and peppers with fresh herbs. The scent roused his hunger. He grasped the Parmesan cheese, a small grater, and a hunk of crusty bread while Emily pulled out the napkins and silverware. "You thought of everything."

"Not the drinks. I hoped—"

"We have coffee, lemonade and soft drinks." She motioned toward the table. "Martin, I'm astounded."

"Don't be." His pulse hitched. "And I'll take a Coke for now." He watched as she strode to the small refrigerator, carried back two drinks and set them on the table. Then she paused beside the chair. "Is this one of those occasions?" A faint smile emerged on her face.

"Every occasion is." Martin shifted behind the desk chair and slipped it beneath her, then seated himself. After asking the blessing, he handed her the serving spoon. "Eat while it's warm."

She placed a portion on her plate, then tore off a piece of the bread.

Martin grated the cheese onto her pasta and did the same for himself. The first bite reassured him, especially seeing an agreeable look on Emily's face. The loneliness he'd been feeling drifted away. "I've missed you these past two weeks."

She lifted her head. "I miss Nessie." She dug into the pasta, following suit with a grin. "And I miss you too."

Her words wrapped around him. Triggered by her response, Martin dug his hand into his pocket. "We haven't been alone since your birthday. Did you realize?"

Her eyes searched his as if looking for his meaning.

"The waiter interrupted us when you were opening your gifts, and—" he pulled the package out of his pocket "—I didn't give you my present."

She straightened, her gaze darting between his face and the wrapped box. "But you gave me the other things and the amazing dinner surprise. That was gift enough."

"Let me decide that." He placed the package on the table and motioned for her to open it.

Emily gazed at it a moment, then at him.

He nodded. "Go ahead. It's not something I can use, and our food is getting cold." He managed to chuckle while his lungs felt empty of air.

She grinned back and drew the gift closer. When she'd removed the ribbon and wrapping, she gazed at the box, her brow furrowing a moment before she lifted the lid. She gasped. "Martin, this is absolutely beautiful." She lifted the bracelet from the velvety interior. Oval pink gemstones set in a gold band glinted in the artificial light. Emily turned it over in her hand, gazing at each nuance of color refracting from the facets. "Pink. So lovely. What are the stones?"

"Tourmaline from Mozambique. They reminded me of you. Delicate and mesmerizing."

As she gazed at the stones again, a quizzical look grew on her face. "Me? Mesmerizing?"

He nodded. "You are. I don't think you see yourself as others do."

"As you do. Most people see me as a bit different." She grinned.

"And that's why you're mesmerizing." He brushed her hand. "Would you like me to hook the bracelet?"

She dangled it in the light. "It's too pretty to wear here, but I don't care." She handed it to him and watched as he clasped it. She modeled her hand in one direction, then the other, a look of admiration filling her face. "I've never owned anything so elegant, but—" Her head snapped up, her expression making a hundred-and-eighty-degree turn. "I'm sure it was too expensive. I shouldn't accept it."

He clasped her hands in his. "Emily, if it were too expensive I wouldn't have purchased it. And besides, you're worth much more to me. You've given me your time and energy with Nessie, far beyond any payment you received, and you've given me something far more important."

Her brows lifted as she searched his face.

"Friendship and your company. It feels strange not seeing you. I'll be glad when Steph's back to work and you can take a break. You work too hard."

She shrugged. "When I love something, I give it my all. I can't do things halfway."

His pulse jumped with her admission. He'd seen it in her behavior, and it was one of the attributes he loved. Devotion was a quality money couldn't buy. He'd never experienced that in his life, at least not the way Emily gave of herself.

He released her hand and picked up his fork, hoping the casserole had remained warm. Only a few dogs' yips and sporadic barks broke the silence while they finished the food. He eyed her bracelet glinting in the light as he savored the meal, but mostly, he relished their time together.

He'd learned from Emily. Lugging the food to the shelter hadn't been convenient, but he'd paid attention to her comment at the hospital. If he wanted to become a man worthy of a lovely woman like Emily, he had decided to take heed.

After she pushed back her plate, Emily leaned back and gazed at him. "That was delicious. Thank you." She eyed the gift again, her eyes twinkling with the same glint. "And the bracelet is gorgeous."

Martin's chest zinged with pleasure before it wrenched with concern. "The thought of you sitting here day in and out without a real meal kills me."

"I know." A thoughtful look filled her face. "I don't know what else to do. Steph's not ready to return to work, and when the baby comes home, she won't be able to for a while."

Though he had much to say on that matter, now wasn't the time. They had so few moments together and that conversation had the potential of causing an argument. But Steph needed to hire more help, and that was that. He left that line of thought, caught in another subject he'd planned to tell her about later. But why not today. She needed a lift. "I've been thinking about my mother."

Concern riffled across her face. "Is anything wrong?"

"No. Nothing like that. In fact, she's doing very well. Nick's been taking her to the house to spend time with Steph. He's afraid she'll be too depressed if he leaves her alone. But it's also been good for Mom. She's different. Vital and getting around as if the stroke hadn't happened."

Awareness shone on Emily's face, and she rested her

elbows on the table. "I told you, she needed a purpose. When she went to the facility, no matter how nice it is, she lost her reason to live a full life. No one there needed her. She was lonely for family, she had lost her identity, in a way."

Bull's-eye. Emily hit the mark. "So I've been thinking."

A look of hope flew to her face. "About...?"

"About where Mom should live." There, he'd said it. His pulse skipped as the words entered the world instead of banging around in his head.

She drew back. "With Nick?"

"No. With me." Now that had made its way into the open, too.

Emily leaned closer, her scowl gone. "Really? You want your mom to live with you?"

He pressed his lips together, seeking words to explain. "It's not perfect. But she needs family. With the baby, Nick has a new responsibility, and I'm a poor example of being the best at visiting."

"Don't say that." She lowered her eyes, but when she looked up excitement lit her face. "Are you going to fix the spare bedroom for her?" She faltered over the last words. "It's a nice room, but, I mean, you could make it more feminine. I'd love to help."

"It's small, and my office isn't much bigger. I'm thinking about—" If he said it now, the idea would come to life. Martin struggled with the words while Emily's gaze probed his. "I'm thinking about looking for a new place. One with a separate apartment with a little sitting room and—"

"Move?" Her eyes widened, but before he could respond, a smile lit her face. "It's a wonderful idea. She'll be thrilled." She captured his hand. "Martin, you're the best son ever."

*The best son ever.* He drank in the words, but another wish filled his heart. If he could only be the best husband ever. It would change his world.

The sound of the baby's cry pulled Emily to her feet. An anxious rush of emotion washed over her as she turned toward Steph. "Want me to check?"

Steph shook her head with a chuckle. "Sure. I get my turn at three in the morning. If you'd like to trade, I'd be—"

Emily brushed her suggestion away with a grin and hurried into the baby's nursery. The tiny form, her arms flailing, looked so small Emily feared breaking her. She reached beneath the baby's head and back as she eased the infant into her arms, amazed at the feeling that wove through her heart. A child. A new life that could be guided through childhood and blossom into a young woman.

Her chest ached with the love she felt. Having watched Steph change Megan's diaper, she checked and followed the process, careful with the delicate limbs and soft flesh. A sensation washed over her, an unbelievable awe that God could create such a wonder.

When she carried Megan to Steph, she'd already prepared to feed the baby, and Emily sat across from her, watching how the sharp-humored Steph had become a gentle, loving mother without lessons, an innate ability held dormant until needed.

"She's changed our lives." Steph's eyes hadn't left her feeding infant. "And for the better."

"I can see that." For the better. The remarkable possibility inched through her mind. How long had she wanted better?

"Nick and I have lost our self-centeredness. We realize what a gift this little girl is to us. God's given her to us to raise and to keep safe so that He can work wonders in her life. Every day I pray that we can make her life better than ours."

"I'd want the same, Steph." Her mind soared back to her family, but she refused to go with it. No more self-pity.

Steph finally lifted her gaze from the baby. "Not money or treasures on earth. I'm talking about having faith, love, compassion, fulfillment. Those kind of qualities."

Faith. Love. And hope. Emily had clung to hope in the last months since meeting Martin. Hope to change. Hope to let go of the baggage she lugged. Hope of having a real family. But hope needed something else, too. Confidence. Trust. Whatever it was she wanted to grasp it and hang on. Steph had hung on. She'd lost a husband to suicide years earlier, and yet she'd pulled herself up. She'd grasped hope and look at her now.

Emily searched her friend's tender gaze. "I hate to admit it, but I envy you."

"No need to envy us. You have the capacity to have a child. Just let go of the fears you have about being married and—"

"Marriage frightens me. I had bad role models, but it's really more than that. It's why it freezes me to the core. What I really can't imagine is opening myself to someone."

"You mean being honest and trusting they'll accept what you tell them?"

Emily digested the question. "We all have things

we regret, and I've always thought two people in love should have an honest and open relationship. Share the bad things as well as the good." She studied Steph's questioning eyes. "Do you know what I mean?"

"I think so." Her frown remained. "You're saying a man and woman should open their souls and spill out all their sins...like a confessional."

"That sounds odd, but sort of." Emily pictured herself in a closet talking through a slit in the wall to an unknown ear. She didn't need a closet since she'd created one of her own, and the Lord listened to her confession.

"The important thing to remember is Jesus washed your sins away, so I'm not sure you have to confess anything. You're a new creation. You're clean and shiny." Steph tilted her head, her face contorting with question. "Do you think I'm wrong?"

Her question struck a chord. "I know I've been forgiven, and I know I'm a new creation, but..." Not being open seemed dishonest.

"I don't know, Steph." She lowered her head. "Maybe each person has to do what seems right."

Steph lifted Megan onto her shoulder and patted her back. "I'll have to think about that, but you have a point."

Silence settled over them. Emily struggled with the idea. How could she make a commitment to someone who didn't know she'd lived part of her life without morals, taking chances and going against everything God stood for. Her chest tightened forcing her to fight for air.

Grateful Steph had been focused on Megan, Emily tucked the subject back into the recesses of her mind.

Her jaw ached from the tension. "I'm sure you're relieved that Molly found someone to help you at the day care."

"You can say that again. How can I thank you for putting in so many hours for me? I know it was difficult, and you look as if you could use a vacation."

The desire whooshed through her chest. "I wish I could."

"Why can't you?"

Money flashed through Emily's thoughts, but she'd stockpiled some while working the long hours. "I don't know." She grinned, feeling her stress lift. "Maybe I can."

"Go for it. I know Martin misses seeing you."

Her pulse jigged. "Did he say something to you?"

She snickered. "Does he have to? It's obvious." Her smile faded to a scowl. "Don't tell me you aren't aware that Martin has feelings for you?"

Emily's pulse skipped. The kiss. It never left her mind, but men kissed women without love. She knew that from experience. "We're friends." That's all she could accept. "I know he likes me."

Steph's familiar eye-rolling preceded her words. "Take another look, Emily. You're an intelligent woman. 'Like' isn't the word." Her grin returned. "Try 'crazy about.'"

Crazy about? The words winged their way into her head. *He's crazy about me.* She searched Steph's face for the barbed look that usually followed her humor. It didn't. But Steph had it all wrong. She and Martin had agreed to be friends. Yet her imagination had taken flight with impossible dreams. And deep inside she wanted more.

Martin crazy about her? No. Steph was the one who was crazy.

# Chapter Thirteen

Emily leaned over Martin's dining table, scooting brochures from one side to the other, trying to decide which house plan she liked best. When she thought one looked perfect, another attracted her more. "I don't know." She looked into Martin's eyes as they searched hers with expectation. She refocused on one of the floor plans again. "You've given me too many choices."

"I need choices. I'm trying to weigh my mother's needs and then mine."

Her heart melted, hearing him mention his mother's needs first. Each time he validated the changes she'd witnessed in him since they'd become friends, her spirit lifted a little more. "Okay, let's cancel the ones we've questioned."

As Martin scooted his chair closer to hers, the scent of his aftershave sailed past, giving her that I'm-home feeling. Each visit, each time together seemed to bond them tighter. Since talking with Steph, Emily had watched his actions, and she had to agree. Martin cared about her and counted on her more each day—not in the kind of way he counted on Nick. That was different. Nick ran errands and came to his rescue, the same way she'd begun her relationship with him. But she'd put her foot down, and from then on, Martin had viewed her with a different perspective. She even sensed it was admiration. Someone admired her. The feeling raced to her chest and lingered there.

While Martin studied the house brochures, she tried to make a list of his needs. "You don't want to lose the things you love about this house."

"Right." He paused a moment. "A large master bedroom. Walk-in closet. Master bath. I want those. A home office is nice. Private area for Mom."

A vision shot to her mind. "And the patio and nice yard."

He slipped his arm around her shoulder and gave it a squeeze. "For flowers."

"Your mother loves them." She sent him a toying look.

"So do you." He leaned closer and kissed the tip of her nose.

The touch tingled all the way to her limbs. "A big kitchen. Formal dining room. And—"

"A place Nessie can call home."

His arm hadn't left her, and she felt his playful hug again, but before another word left her mouth, Nessie pattered across the carpet, wagging her tail, and gazed at them with a let's-go-out-and-play look.

Martin slipped his arm away and bent down to scratch Nessie's ears. "Not now, little girl." He grinned. "Poor thing, I should let her out." He rose and headed for the patio door.

With him gone, Emily selected three of her favorite houses. He'd looked at a couple of new models and then a used home that provided a layout of the house with details. All three had qualities Martin wanted.

He wandered back through the doorway, looking as if he'd prefer to be running around with Nessie, and Emily rose to meet him. "Here are my favorites, I think. It's hard to tell from a brochure."

Martin gave the floor plans a cursory look, then tossed them back on the table. "I like those two, but what you said gives me an idea. You're right. A brochure doesn't give the full picture."

He looked at her as if he'd said something brilliant, and she chuckled.

"That's not all." He shot her a playful wink. "Let's take a day off work and have a house-hunting day. You know my mom and what she'd like."

The idea excited her. She would be part of his decision, looking at elegant homes she would never see otherwise. "I'd love it. Steph asked me why I didn't take a vacation. One day is better than none."

"You deserve a week. Two weeks." He shifted closer, his eyes searching hers with a look that fluttered through her chest.

The sensation stopped her breathing as she drowned in his eyes. When he drew her closer, weakness overcame her, and she tried to conquer the amazing feelings with no success. Martin's hand rose up her back to her hair, and his fingers wove into the strands with a gentle touch like a breeze.

His breath heightened, and she gave way to the emotion, greeting his mouth as it met hers, his lips tender, yet demanding. The world spun away from her, and she was lost in his arms. As he drew back, his eyes questioned hers, and she couldn't deny the answer. She was falling for him in some crazy whirlwind way that she'd tried to deny.

Martin slipped his arms lower around her waist, his fingers knotted behind her, his gaze sweeping from her hair to her lips to her eyes. "I've wanted to do that for so long."

She swallowed, not finding words to answer back. Instead she answered with her hand, placing it on his cheek and speaking with her presence. She'd stopped running.

Martin closed his eyes and turned his head to her hand. His warm lips brushed a kiss on her fingers.

Nessie barked, drawing them both back to reality. Martin released her with a feeble shrug and headed back to the patio door while Emily lingered, savoring the feel of his mouth on hers and asking the Lord for courage to trust Martin.


The smell of burgers drifted from the grill, and Martin chuckled at Nick fussing over Megan. Though she was over a month old, she was so small she still looked like a newborn. But she'd received the hospital's stamp of approval for being ready to face the world.

Fred and Suzette had romped around the family until everyone had found seats on the deck. Then the dogs wandered away to a shady spot beneath the trees. They reminded Martin of an old married couple comfortable with each other and with their life together.

The women were inside putting the rest of the Fourth of July meal together. Emily had even baked a cake at his house. She followed the recipe to the letter, and Martin saw her pride when she pulled out the plump layers of homemade cake. She'd refused to use a box as he would have done. His mom had gloated too since the recipe had been hers.

Three days earlier when he'd dropped every restraint and kissed Emily the way he'd long to, he'd relived the experience. She'd leaned into the kiss, but in her eyes, he still saw her hesitation. The look had slithered down his back as if she'd dropped an ice cube down his shirt. Emily's responses to him wavered and he longed to know the reason. He'd told himself she'd accepted friendship and ended it there, but not when he kissed her. The kiss she returned negated that notion. He had enough brains to know he couldn't rush her. Time would tell. Though patience wasn't his virtue, he worked at it, holding each positive moment with Emily as a treasure.

When he watched her with Megan, his heart lifted. Though she insisted she lacked the attributes of being a homemaker, he recognized the innate ability to be a mother. And she'd grown in comfort around the house, too. Occasionally she'd had the courage to try another recipe when she'd visited, and she knew home decorating. They'd talked about the houses he'd looked at, and she had great ideas. He couldn't wait to take her to look at the homes they both liked and see her reaction. A new house meant more to him than a place for his mother, though that had been his motivation. It would have empty rooms, rooms that could be a nursery, and he could only picture Emily as the one rocking the cradle.

He flipped the burger, his heart pitching as well when he realized the dreams that one kiss could encourage.

Emily stepped through the doorway onto Nick's deck and stepped down to the lawn, but not before leaning over to gaze at Megan. The look in her eyes made his heart swell. Nessie followed Emily as she headed toward him. The dog adored her. So did he, but the terrier had a straightforward way of showing it. He wished he had a tail to wag. Picturing that, he grinned.

"What's so funny?"

He shook his head. "Thinking about Megan and family. Good things make me smile."

"Me, too." She stood beside him, her gaze on the burgers. "We're done inside. Salads are ready, condiments, buns, and my cake." The corners of her mouth curved upward.

Her cake. She'd swirled blueberry and raspberry Jell-O into the batter, and he expected it to get oohs and aahs from the family when they cut into it.

"Let's not talk about the house hunting, okay?"

She gave him a quizzical look.

"Did you tell someone already? I'd wanted to surprise—"

"No. I thought you should tell your mom. I know it's a surprise."

"Let's keep it that way for a while." He pulled a burger from the grate and set it on the warmer. "We can tell her once everything's settled."

Her eyes brightened. "Good idea. I thought maybe you were getting cold feet."

"Not even a toe. I'm excited. This is one of my best decisions."

She gave him a poke. "What's the other?"

His heartbeat tripped over itself. *Loving you.* But he couldn't speak it. Not yet. "Getting Nessie."

She laughed, but he noticed a flash of disappointment.

"That's when I met you." He brushed his finger along her arm.

It took a second before she raised her eyes to his. "I liked that decision, too."

His pulse danced. "These are ready."

Emily spun around and headed inside while he lifted the platter and followed. He watched his step since Fred and Suzette bounded beside him, their noses lifting at the smell of the burgers.

Seated around the dining room table, Martin studied his family's interaction with the two new additions, Emily and Megan. They both fit in as if they'd always been there. Although he occasionally got one of those admit-you've-fallen-in-love looks from Nick and Steph, he'd tried to play it cool. He had failed, but he'd made a valiant effort. He hoped eventually Emily would catch on before he admitted his feeling aloud. Though she appeared aware of everything else, how he felt about her seemed to fly past her.

When they'd finished eating, everyone agreed to wait a bit for dessert. Steph rose first to change Megan's diaper, and when she returned to the table, she headed for him. "It's your turn."

She held out her arms, and Martin eyed the baby with awe. "You want me to hold her?"

Steph rolled her eyes. "No, I'm standing here for my health." A grin followed. "I want to see what you'd look like as a father."

Father. His pulse skipped. He noticed everyone watching to see what he would do, but most of all, Emily's expression swept over him. Tenderness etched her face when she gazed at him, and her eyes encouraged him to open his arms. He did, allowing Steph to nestle Megan against his chest.

The child seemed as light as a throw pillow. Her minute fist flexed open, then closed again as she tucked it beneath her chin. Megan had Steph's coloring but he could see the Davis eyes. Not the color, because hers looked blue, but the line and shape of the eyes. He could picture her sweeping brow when her hair finally made an appearance.

Emily leaned closer, her eyes shifting from the baby to his face. "It looks good on you." Her voice was a whisper.

His chest tightened, imagining how he might feel if this child were his. If he'd learned anything, he would be a good father. That would be his daily prayer. He looked at Megan again, emotions charging through him and winning the battle. In desperation, he swallowed the knot in his throat. "Would you like a turn?"

Emily's gaze washed over him, making him weak. Finally she nodded and lifted Megan from his arms as if she'd been toting babies forever.

Tension left his back. Despite the amazing feel, the emotions were too real. The tiny form in his arms. A new life from the love of his brother and Steph. He forced the emotion to pass, grasping for anything to change the subject. "Who's in for fireworks tonight?" He eyed his watch.

"Fireworks, where?" Nick rose and scooted back his chair. "Rochester Hills had theirs a couple days ago."

Martin slid his chair back. "Stony Creek."

Emily glanced at him. "Over the water. That would be pretty."

His mother rose and gathered the plates. "That's too late for me."

"Sounds like fun, but we can't go this year." Nick made a sweeping gesture toward Megan. "She's too young for that."

Martin figured as much. "How about you?" He captured Emily's gaze.

Her eyes sparkled as much as the birthday bracelet she'd worn today. "I'd love to."

That's what he wanted to hear. Alone with the fireworks above them, he hoped to tell her about the skyrockets in his heart.

Parking had proved nearly impossible at Stoney Creek Park, until someone finally pulled from a spot—a total surprise to Emily—and Martin pulled in. She waited until Martin opened her door. She'd learned to let him be nice to her. He had seemed quiet once they'd turned off Tienken Road onto Washington Road. Apparently something had roused his thoughts.

Walking in silence toward the picnic area, Martin wove his fingers around hers. He gave her hand a squeeze yet said nothing.

The day had been wonderful. Sharing a holiday celebration with a family had been beyond any of her expectations. With her family, holidays had come and gone like any other day, except her parents sometimes were more drunk. That meant they also argued more.

Her chest tightened picturing Nick and Steph's happiness. Megan gained ground each day, and the pediatrician felt her premature birth wouldn't leave any lasting effect. Emily admired her friends' faith. Theirs provided an example of what God could do.

The vision of Martin holding the baby swam in her mind. In her wildest dreams, she could never have imagined the delight it gave her. He acted nervous and uncertain. Yet he'd nestled the child against him, and the glow on his face amazed her. He would make a wonderful father someday.

Along with her growing contentment, she continued to ache. Until she dealt with her issues, nothing would change, and the longer she stayed connected to Martin and his family the more difficult it would be to walk away. No matter how often she reminded herself she was a new creation, she still pictured herself as a valuable antique plate, its broken pieces glued together. Though it resembled the original dish, it no longer had the same value.

"How's this?"

The sound of his voice jarred her. They stood on a grassy spot some distance from the water, and since the picnic tables were filled, she nodded. Martin tossed a blanket he'd carried from the car onto the ground.

She sank to one side, and he sat beside her. The sun had lowered on the horizon, but the day's warmth still radiated from the earth. She slid down, stretching out on her side and plucked at the blades of grass. "You're quiet."

"Just thoughtful, I guess."

She'd already figured that out. His response added nothing to ease her concern. "I enjoyed the day very much. I'm glad you invited me."

"My family likes you, and you like them, I think."

A warm sensation settled in her chest. "You know I do." She searched his face, noticing tension creeping into his jaw.

Martin eyed his watch, then straightened his back. "Looks like a late sunset. They're supposed to have the fireworks at ten, but it could be later."

Emily tossed the grass blades onto the lawn and pulled herself up to a seated position, her legs folded in front of her. "We didn't have to come tonight."

His gaze softened. "No, I wanted to. We can use the time alone."

*Time alone.* As if the sun had plunged below the

horizon, the warmth vanished, and instead ice prickled her skin. "What's wrong, Martin?"

He drew in a lengthy breath before he shook his head. "I'm confused. That's all."

She searched his face, her heart squeezed with speculation. "Is this about me?"

"Us." He reached toward her and clasped her hand. "We kissed the other day, and—" He looked away.

"I remember."

His head turned toward her, confusion written on his face. "I hoped that you would."

She'd wanted the comment to be lighthearted, but it had failed. "Are you sorry about the kiss?"

"No. Are you?"

"It meant the world to me." Her mind whirred, having no idea where the crazy conversation was headed or why it had even begun.

"Emily, I need to know where we stand. We've agreed to be friends, but...friends don't kiss. Not that way. I've stepped out of my comfort zone since I met you. For years, I'd kept myself from having strong feelings about anyone, but I do now, and I can't keep hiding them."

Her head swam with words she wanted to say, emotions she longed to express, but the battle raged between her head and heart, and no matter which way it went, she couldn't win. "I care about you, Martin. Know that I do."

"But you have doubts about me." He lowered his head.

His distress tugged at her. "Not you. I doubt me." As if she'd eaten sand, Emily licked her dry lips. "You're important to me. I don't want to lose what we have, but I'm not sure I'm ready. It's hard to explain."

His eyes searched hers. "My intentions are honorable,

Emily. I'm not trifling with your feelings and I'd never hurt you intentionally."

She pressed her palm against his cheek. "I know that." She drew closer. " I know Denise hurt you when she left, and you're still scarred from that. You've questioned whether or not you'd ever be worthy of another woman. But I do believe with all my heart that you will make a wonderful husband and father. But I'm not sure…"

The look in his eyes tore her heart.

"I'm not sure I can be a wife. It's complicated, and I'm trying to sort it out." Her eyes blurred with tears in the near dark. In the shadows, Martin's handsome face looked haggard. Deep creases marred his smooth brow, and his eyes appeared to have sunken into darkness.

His hand cradled hers. "Are you willing to give it time? I'll wait if there's hope."

She swallowed, ready to make a promise she didn't know if she could keep. "Give me a few more days. Let me think this through. I'll try to make sense out of the things inside me, and then I'll have an answer."

Gazing into the darkened sky, he bit the edge of his lip, then inched his eyes to hers. "You're worth the wait. Just promise me you'll make it soon, and until then let's forget this conversation. Can we do that?"

With her heart in a vise, she nodded. "Just like always. Best friends."

He leaned closer, his eyes asking. She tilted her lips to his with her answer. As if her heart had wings, it flew into the darkened sky into a burst of colorful sparkles.

Martin drew back, his gaze saying more than she'd ever dreamed. They turned their faces to the fireworks display. Yet deep inside, Emily's own skyrockets illuminated her thoughts. If she wanted happiness with the man who'd said everything except the words "I love you," she had to take a chance. She had to trust and give her fears to the Lord.

She had to.

## Chapter Fourteen

"What do you think?" Martin stood beside Emily with his hands in his pockets, eyeing the second house they'd viewed that day. He'd come to rely on Emily's judgment. "The other house was too modern. We both agree on that. This one's traditional."

"I love the big kitchen and the huge breakfast area, but—" She curled her nose and grinned. "The patio is small, and I'm not crazy about the step-down dining room. I can see your mother falling in there."

"It's just like you. I hadn't thought of that, plus I'd want to move the study to the front bedroom and then open the study area so Mom could have a sitting room too." Emily had worried about being a wife, but he had no trouble envisioning it. She had an eye for decorating, and now she could cook and did a great job. She'd even become inventive with recipes.

He slipped his arms around her waist and pulled her close. "I'd make a mess of this by myself. I need you to see the logical things I miss."

She tipped her head upward. "You'd do fine."

The urge to kiss her swept over him, and he lowered

his lips to hers, tilted so welcoming as if waiting for him.

Emily kissed him back with a naturalness that left him breathless. He'd feared their talk would push her away, but it had drawn them closer in a strange way. The pins-and-needles situation still hung over his head, but he had convinced himself to trust Emily's decision, and he'd prayed that God would work in both of them. He didn't want another mistake in his life, but his heart told him this relationship was heaven-blessed.

When he drew back, her eyes were heavy-lidded, and his heart skipped with her response to the kiss. "We have one more house to look at." He forced himself to keep his mind on their house hunting. "Want to?"

"I do." She slipped her hand in his.

*I do.* Two small words prickled down his arms. One day he longed to hear her say those words in front of their family, friends and their minister. He could picture her as a bride. He'd watched her grow and change, and in the back of his mind, he saw it all as a bride in training, just as he'd been in training to be a better man. He chuckled.

She faltered and eyed him. "What's so funny?"

He shrugged. "I'm thinking about how Steph and you often say dogs have attributes people should have, and I was thinking how people benefit from training just like pets."

"What made you think of that?" She gave him a curious look.

He tried to guide her toward the door but she stood still. "Look at me. I'm better for what I've learned. You trained Nessie and me at the same time."

A grin sprouted on her face. "Good boy." She patted his cheek. "Sorry I don't have a treat."

"Sure you do." He kissed her again.

Something had happened since the talk that he couldn't comprehend. He sensed relief for both of them that they'd settled on the same page of a suspense novel. They knew where they were going but the mystery hadn't been resolved yet. But like all good novels, Martin counted on a happy ending.

They left the house and met the Realtor who'd waited outside after their first walk-through. Giving them private time took away the pressure. He held the door for Emily who'd finally accepted his gentlemanly ways, and he settled into the passenger seat beside the woman. As they drove he reviewed the house plan, his excitement growing.

When they arrived, Emily joined his enthusiasm. "I love the outside. Look at the covered porch and all the flowers."

Flowers. For a man who'd never given a hoot for flowers, he'd certainly learned to appreciate them. He slipped from the car and opened her door. Hand in hand, they stood back, admiring the brick home with an attached garage that looked like an extension of the house. He wished it were closer to his business, though being on one level made it perfect for his mother. "So far so good."

The Realtor unlocked the door and motioned them inside. The entry led into a large living room with a fireplace and an amazing dining area with built-in cabinets along one wall.

"It's like the layout you have now, but bigger. I like it."

The huge kitchen offered counter space that Emily loved and a counter that connected with a massive family room with vaulted ceiling and a raised hearth with a second fireplace. He watched Emily's gaze shift from one side to the other, a smile growing on her face. She hurried ahead to the French doors to the side and turned to face him. "A huge deck. I love it."

The Realtor beckoned. "The large guest room also looks out onto the deck. Follow me."

Martin wove his fingers through Emily's, and followed the woman. In the guest room doorway, they both stopped. God had answered his prayers. A bedroom with a walk-in closet and a sitting room with a sliding door to the deck. "This is perfect for my mom."

Emily squeezed his hand. "She'll love it." She wandered in, and he followed, checking the large bathroom with tub and shower.

As if God had guided them, the rest of the house met his needs. Another guest room, laundry area and on the other side of the house beyond the living area stood a den with built-in shelving and a bay window along with a master suite with a sitting room, walk-in closet and a huge bath. He gazed at Emily imagining how much she would enjoy the space.

He didn't have to ask what she thought. She stood in the middle of the room, turning around, her eyes wide and her mouth posed in amazement. She headed for another set of French doors and when she looked out, she spun around. "Look. You have to see this."

She opened the door and stepped out as he followed. The large porch wrapped around the length of the house and outside the master suite, the builder had added a sunken spa.

The Realtor joined them. "It has a deck panel that covers it for cooler days and makes it usable floor space."

Martin could only shake his head and tilt it Heavenward,

sending up a thank You to the Lord for leading him to a perfect house. From Emily's expression, he knew he didn't have to ask. She loved it too.

The woman vanished again, leaving them alone, and Martin drew Emily close, his heart smacking against his breastbone. He gazed into her eyes, wanting to have her say she would be his wife but the words didn't come. Yet his confidence grew each day, recalling that the Lord could accomplish more than he could ever hope and dream. He'd finally put it in the Lord's hands.

His hope for a house close to his work vanished with Emily's excitement. Her eyes said what his wisdom knew. "This is it."

She slipped her arms around his waist and pressed her head against his chest. "It is. It's perfect. Your mom will love it here."

"Would you?" He held his breath.

But Emily inched her head upward and smiled. "Any woman would love this home, Martin. It's a family house, ready for love and laughter." She gazed into the large backyard. "And ready for children."

This time he struggled to breathe. *Children.* Emily. *Lord, I trust in You.*

"You'll buy it?" Her voice seemed a whisper.

He nodded. "I'll put an offer in today. And then my house can go on the market." He noticed her questioning look. "I know the market is slow, but I don't need the money from the house to make a down payment on this one."

She closed her eyes and opened them, as if trying to grasp what he'd said. God had blessed him. He had finances. What he needed was love. The forever kind.

Emily stood in the new kitchen, eyeing the cabinets and counters now filled with Martin's dishes and appliances. She heard him in the master bedroom, hanging his clothes and shifting boxes, even furniture. He seemed as bad as she was about making decisions about where things should go.

She wandered down the hallway and stood in the doorway of Julia's room, thrilled Martin had given her full rein on decorating for his mom. Instead of the light beige walls Julia had at her condo, Emily had convinced Martin to have the bedroom area painted a pastel green, the color of the first buds of spring. When she'd visited Julia not long ago, she'd noticed her bedspread, and the color she'd chosen matched perfectly. She'd added a floral border below the ceiling and created a bouquet of silk flowers that she could set on her dresser or table. She'd taken a chance with the sitting room, but knowing Julia's glowing spirit, Emily had been inspired by a sunset and chose a soft coral that added a cozy warmth to the room. And Martin had purchased a recliner for her in a burnished coral shade. Perfect with the wall coloring. Her heart felt full picturing Julia's face. Martin had insisted on keeping it a surprise.

But now the house was nearly ready for their housewarming dinner. Little more than two weeks had passed since Martin had made his offer, and the best news he'd received was a bid on his present home. In a couple more days, he'd complete the move into this new house.

Her promise to Martin had been the only weight she'd carried since they'd talked. He cared deeply for her. He'd been open, and she felt the same. She'd prayed and fought her fears until she faced her options. She stood at two roads—one she knew, life as it was, and one would be a leap of faith, a new path that could lead to happiness or disaster if he rejected her once he knew the whole story. She would never know until she took the step.

Her hands trembled, and she tucked them into her pockets. She'd told herself that today would be the day, the day to embrace life with hope or to cling to life without it. The decision had become clear.

"Where are you?"

Martin's voice sailed down the hall, and Emily retraced her steps to the kitchen, her fingers knotted in her pockets, her heart ready to be laid bare. If their relationship was to be tested, today was the day.

She entered the kitchen and spotted Martin standing in the entrance to the family room. When he turned a smile brightened his face. "There you are."

"I was looking at your mom's suite. I hope she likes it."

"She'll love it." He met her at the corner of the counter wall and drew her into his arms. "Is that what you're worried about?"

"Worried? No. I'm just a little anxious." She'd already guessed that he'd noticed stress on her face. She hadn't been able to hide much from Martin lately. He seemed to read her moods very well.

"You like the house?" He searched her eyes.

His concern spattered her with guilt. "I love it. I've told you."

"Then it's something else." He drew back, his gaze probing hers.

She pulled her hands from her pockets and rested them on his chest, unable to speak.

Martin covered them with his palm. "Tell me what it is?"

Anxiety flashed across his face, and she wished she could smile to relieve his worry, but the raw emotion careening through her denied her the ability. "It's the talk you've wanted."

"The talk?" For a second, he looked blank until understanding registered on his face. "Your answer about where we go from here."

"Yes." The tremors spread from her hands to her legs, and her lungs collapsed against the wall of her chest. "I need to explain everything." She grasped for air.

"Today? Now?" His arms supported her.

She nodded.

"You need to sit, Emily, before you fall over." Though he'd tried to lighten his tone, his stress couldn't be hidden. He wrapped his arm around her back and guided her across the room to the sofa facing the fireplace. He sat beside her, and when she looked up, she noticed Nessie had found her home, a cozy spot between the French doors and the raised hearth. In that spot, the dog had the best of both worlds, warmth from the fireplace or the sun. Emily longed for that warmth, a cozy spot called home.

With her heart in her throat, she shifted to face him. Sorrow spilled from her. Sorrow that she'd caused Martin's worried expression and sorrow for her indecision. She gazed into his expressive eyes, and beneath his distress, she saw love. Tears sprang to her eyes as the words formed on her lips. "You've opened your heart to me, and it's one of those impossible dreams that I thought could never come true."

He slipped his hands into hers, his eyes seeking her answer.

"My feelings have been the same as yours."

A flash of assurance lit his face.

"But you don't really know me, and that's been the problem. I'm not the woman you think I am."

His brow darkened, and she heard his intake of breath. "You're not Emily Ireland?"

Normally she would have chuckled, but no laughter came. "That's not what I mean. You've said wonderful things to me and called me fresh and special." Her throat caught. "I'm not fresh. I'm rotten inside."

"Rotten. No. That doesn't make sense." His eyes searched hers.

"Let me explain." She struggled to get her thoughts in order, her chest so tight her lungs felt compressed. Words whirred inside her, and she grasped them trying to make sense out of the barrage of images. "I talked with Steph a while back about being open and honest with any man if I ever fell in love. She said I had been forgiven by God and my sins were gone." She studied his face, seeing more than concern in his eyes. "But they're not gone. They're right here." She struck her chest with her palm. "And I can't get rid of them."

Confusion sparked in his eyes. "I don't understand."

"It's about my past. It's things I did. Things I'm ashamed of that happened before I knew the Lord, but I knew better even then."

Martin's head swiveled like a searchlight sweeping the sky. "It's passed, Emily. You don't have to tell me unless—"

"I have to. Don't you understand?" Her tears broke free and rolled down her cheeks. She swiped them away, frustrated with her weakness, her fear of the truth. "It makes a difference, Martin. I want you to know the real me."

"I do know the real you." A tender look softened the stress in his face. "I love the you that I know."

"But a committed relationship has to begin with honesty and trust. What if you heard this from someone else." She shook her head. "I don't know who, but what if? You'd be hurt. Devastated."

Air drained from his lungs, and he fell back against the cushion. "Then tell me. Please. But it won't make one bit of difference to me."

But it had made a difference to her. She'd lost respect for herself. She'd felt unworthy of good things. It did make a difference.

Exhausted, Emily lowered her head and pulled her thoughts together. "You know about my family life. I don't have to tell you that, and though I hated what I saw at home, it was the only example I had to follow. I wanted love. I wanted to be loved, and I wanted it desperately. But how does a teenager receive love? What can she do to be loved?"

Martin's eyes searched hers. He shook his head. "I don't know. I was loved and didn't recognize it."

She nodded, knowing his story, his longing to stand out in his parents' eyes, his envy of Nick. He'd struggled as she'd done but in a different way. And he knew the Lord. Refocusing, she lowered her head. "I heard girls talk about making love. Love. That's what I wanted, and that's what I went after."

Martin flinched as a ragged breath escaped him.

"But that didn't help. If that was love, it wasn't the love I wanted, but I didn't stop. One day I believed I would find the love I longed for, but it didn't happen. I started drinking to cover the depression that followed each of the encounters. Bitter. Degrading. Empty. Alcohol washed away the dirtiness I felt until I woke the next day with a headache. Still dirty. Still alone."

"Emily, you were young. You—"

"Martin, let me finish, because it explains something else." Her chest ached from the pounding of her heart.

He gave a fleeting nod and drew her hand into his, his fingers weaving through hers.

"One day I woke with money on my dresser." Pain shot down her arms. "He'd thought I was a prostitute." She lowered her face in her hands, willing herself to grasp control of her emotions. "All I wanted was love. And it happened again. Another man slipped twenty dollars into my hand. I took it, Martin." She lost the battle. Tears swept over her, drowning her in years of shame and guilt.

Martin reached for her, but she pulled back. The rejection flashed on his face.

"Please. Just one more thing. Do you remember the day I came to the house with the gifts for Nessie?"

He nodded.

"You reached into your wallet to pay me and—"

Martin's hand flew to his mouth.

"You didn't know, but that day it all hit me. The pain of my past flooded me, and it made me know that I could never love a man because he could never accept who I am."

"Who you were, Emily? That person's gone." Martin encircled her in his arms and drew her against his chest. His heart pounded against hers, but his hand glided across her back in tender sweeps while he whispered his love in her ear. All the dread she'd carried for so long, all the feeble attempts to lay her baggage at Jesus' feet, all the longing she'd carried wanting only to be loved swept past her, lifting the weight of degradation from her body.

When she'd calmed, Martin captured her chin in his hand. His eyes moist with his own tears sought hers with a tenderness she'd never known. "Emily, when we first met, words came to mind that described you. Fresh, innocent, lovely. I still see those qualities in you. God reads our hearts, and He sees our sorrow and pain.

Those things that happened were lifted from you the day you gave your heart to Jesus. Nothing you've done will change my mind. You're pure in my eyes."

Pure. The word floated into her mind and through her senses. Pure. Clean. Perfect. She searched his eyes, and in them, she saw what she'd looked for her whole life. Love.

"Martin." His name whispered from the depths of her soul.

His gaze captured hers.

"I fell in love with you in those first couple of weeks we met. I was afraid because you are everything any woman could want and—"

"You told me that, but I could never see it. I felt I had nothing to offer."

She remembered the day, the look in his eyes. "It was the day you told me about Denise."

His hand slid to her cheek, cupping it in his warm palm. "It's the day I told you everything. I needed to get rid of it in the same way you needed to rid yourself of the wound you'd carried all these years."

"I have no other secrets." She brushed stray tears from her eyes. "That's all of me—a woman who's wanted love and never found it." She gazed into his eyes. "Until now."

He touched her cheek, wiping away the moisture as his gaze searched hers. "You are beautiful inside and out. I love you, Emily and promise I always will."

His mouth lowered to hers, and she welcomed his lips with her own, willing, yielding, with every ounce of honesty and trust within her.

# *Chapter Fifteen*

"I thought they'd be here by now." Martin stood in the living room window, eyeing the driveway.

Emily grasped his arm. "You're as excited as I am."

He could smell the lemon scent of soap from the kitchen dispenser. She'd buffed and polished every counter and dusted furniture all day Saturday. "It's a double celebration, you know."

She gave him a curious look and he wanted to kick himself. He thought fast. "Showing off the new house and telling Mom we have a place for her."

Her grin broadened to a full smile. Crooked tooth and all.

Martin loved what she thought was a flaw. Hiding things never worked. He and Emily had both learned that lesson. Hiding only magnified the problem and it became a festering wound. He turned his gaze to Emily's beautiful face. Nothing had changed. Her dismal story left him loving her more for her strength and will to overcome the past. Now it was gone and the release had opened doors to an exciting future. A future for them both.

A car door slammed, and Martin turned his attention to the driveway. Nick helped Steph from the car with Megan in her arms, then opened the trunk for a portable basinet. Steph called it a Moses basket. Soon Megan would be too big to use the little bed. As Martin walked into the foyer to greet them, he raised a prayer thanking God for the healthy baby and his brother's happiness.

"Welcome to the new house."

Nick held the door for Steph, and she came in, her gaze flying in one direction and another. "Martin, it's beautiful." She studied the family room, then turned back to the living and dining rooms. "And huge."

Emily headed for her, opening her arms to Megan, and Steph slipped the baby into them with a grin. "It looks good on you."

Instead of denying it, for once Emily chuckled. "I love babies." She carried Megan into the family room and Nick followed with the Moses basket.

When Nessie saw the basket, she hovered around it until Martin came to the rescue. "Nessie, that's Megan's. Your spot is here." He guided the dog to her bed, and she stared at it a moment before sitting beside it, but she kept a curious gaze on the baby.

With that problem resolved, Martin faced a slither of disappointment. "Where's Mom?" He pivoted and eyed the front door. "She's not sick I hope."

Nick chuckled. "She has a date."

"A date?" He looked from Nick to Steph.

"Nick." Steph gave him a swat. "You invited Mike, so he volunteered to pick her up."

"Really." A strange sensation trickled through him.

"Didn't you hear?" Nick's eyebrow arched. "After he came to the Fourth of July celebration, he invited Mom to dinner, and another evening I think they went to the movies."

"Mom?" His chest tightened. "And Mike?"

Steph broke into a laugh. "You sound like a father worried about your daughter's first date. They're adults. It gives them something to do. Someone to be with. I don't think it's a romance, exactly."

He thought of his "friendship" with Emily. He glanced down the hallway, wondering if the rooms he decorated for his mother would be a welcome surprise or was her friendship going to take the same road as his had with Emily.

Nick ambled past him and slipped his arm around Martin's shoulder. "Let her have fun. That's all it is, and I think it's nice."

Emily grinned. "I do too. Life's too long to be lonely." She gave Martin a pointed look, and he closed his mouth. Once again, Emily provided him with common sense.

The doorbell sounded, and Nessie dashed toward the door nearly tripping Martin as he headed down the hallway. When he opened the door, his mom's face glowed.

"The outside is lovely, and the wrap around porch is so unique. I'm happy for you." As he leaned over to kiss her cheek, she tilted her cheek upward before handing him a wrapped gift. "Just a little something for the house."

"Thanks, Mom." He jutted his free hand toward Mike who followed his mother through the door. "Thanks for picking up Mom."

"No problem. It's on the way."

It was, he recalled. His mother had stopped in front of the living room fireplace and looked into the two rooms.

"I like this, especially the built-in buffet in the dining room. That's a great idea."

"I'll give you the grand tour later." He beckoned her to follow him into the family room.

With everyone settled, Martin's nerves took over. He'd given his plan much thought and today seemed perfect for his surprise. His mother cuddled Megan while Nick and Mike appeared to be studying the built-in entertainment center near the fireplace. Emily had vanished into the kitchen with Steph, where he supposed they were checking on the meal and talking about the surprise for his mother.

He watched them, grateful for his loving family and for the Lord's blessings on his life. He'd started a new adventure when he met Emily. She'd helped bring out things in him he never knew were there, and his envy for Nick had passed. In its place, he felt love, and nothing felt better.

Martin shifted to look into the kitchen. Steph had a tray in her hand, and when Emily turned, she had another. Appetizers, he guessed. Emily had latched on to cooking with the excitement of a child with a new bike. Hors d'oeuvres had been added to her list of new discoveries.

The women carried in the trays with the appetizers, plates and napkins and set them on a table. Emily's gaze flicked from one to the other as she checked to make sure everyone had gotten a beverage.

His hands grew clammy, sensing today was the day and the time was right. He walked into the center of the room and drew in a breath.

"Okay, I can tell Martin's ready to give us the ten-dollar tour." Nick grinned.

"First, open my gift." His mother's voice rose above Nick's.

He'd almost forgotten in the confusion. Martin lifted the package from the table where he'd placed it. He noticed Emily eyeing the package, but she stayed where she'd been. He pulled off the ribbon and tore away the wrapping paper, then set the box back on the table to open the lid. His chest tightened when he saw the gift. "Mom, you shouldn't have given me this." He pulled out the vase she'd treasured for so long, the vase his father had given her. "What will you use for your flowers?"

"I have others." She offered a gentle smile. "We had a good talk that day, and I just wanted you to have it."

He clutched the vase to his chest, touched by her willingness to give him something she treasured. He walked to his mother's side and kissed her forehead. "Thanks. This means a great deal to me." He returned the vase to the box for safekeeping.

"Okay, let's get this tour on the road." Nick chuckled.

Martin's lungs emptied. He wiped his hands on his pant legs and acquiesced. He managed a grin, and beckoned everyone to follow.

Emily looked disappointed. She eyed her appetizers and shrugged. Her opportunity to shine would have to wait, too. Nick's eagerness to see his mother's reaction to her new rooms had won out.

Mike gave Julia a hand, and Nick took the baby as Steph rose.

Martin motioned around the room. "You've seen the center of the house. So let's go down the hall."

He led them into the master suite area. They passed his den and then into his room.

"And look here." Emily hurried to the French doors and gave a tour of the sunken tub and the yard.

Nessie had joined her while Martin stood inside, feeling the ring box in his pocket. With this delay he feared dinner would come first. As the family's voice drew nearer, he reorganized his plan. Maybe later was better.

Once his mother had returned inside, her smile growing with each new discovery, Martin's chest constricted as he led them to the other wing of the house. "Not much over here," he said, swallowing his joy. "Down this hallway is the utility room, door to the garage and a guest bedroom." He kept his back to the big surprise.

His mother was the first to return, and as the others filed back, offering their good wishes on the new house, Martin motioned to the door. "Mom, check that room."

She turned the knob and stepped inside. Others followed, and Martin stood in the doorway while they gazed around, no one saying anything except Julia, who praised the lovely colors and decor. Finally, she spotted the sitting-room recliner and faced toward Martin. "This is like a little apartment."

Nick swallowed his laugh. "In some of the real estate brochures, they call this an in-law apartment."

A scowl wavered on her face. "In-laws, but you don't have any."

He stepped closer and put his arm around her trim frame. "But I have a Mom."

She gazed up at him. "Well, I know that."

Everyone laughed while she stared at him, awareness growing like a seed planted in spring. Very slowly.

"Martin, do you mean...?" She pressed her hand against her chest.

He nodded as he embraced her. "We all decided you should be here with me." His earlier worry skittered back into his mind, and he flashed a look at Mike. "If you want to live here."

She clapped her hands together. "Why wouldn't I? This is wonderful. A sitting room and bedroom."

"And your own entrance to the yard." Emily scurried past and opened the French doors.

Julia turned and put her hand to her mouth. "And a place we can plant flowers."

"We?" Martin arched his eyebrow, as a new plan slid into place. "I hope you have an assistant in mind other than me."

She drew Emily to her side. "Emily loves to plant flowers." Her eyes glowed as she looked into Emily's face.

Martin's heart lurched. "She's a good choice."

Emily shot him a quizzical look, and Martin knew the time had come. He closed the distance between them and placed her left hand in his. "Emily said she loves to feel the earth on these lovely fingers, so she really is the perfect choice."

"Then we've all agreed." Julia lowered her arms and grinned at the family, but they were looking at Martin with expectation on their faces. Julia faced him. "Is something wrong?"

"Only one thing." Martin motioned to Emily. "Emily hasn't agreed. You see, I have a big home and a lot of places for flowers, but she's not a gardener."

Nick gave him a wink, then glanced at Steph, as if he realized what was coming.

Martin slipped his free hand into his pocket. "So I've been thinking that with all this space and yard, and with

Nessie adoring Emily…" He captured her gaze. "You know she cries when you leave."

Emily's eyes widened. "She does?"

Martin nodded. "And I miss you too. So I was thinking…"

He knelt on the floor in front of her, her hand still in his. "I'd love to have you stay here always…as my wife."

An intake of air proceeded Steph's exuberance. "Wife! Say yes, Emily."

The room buzzed as Emily's grin grew to a smile. "I've fallen in love with this house and this family." She looked down at Nessie who'd appeared as if wanting to be part of the commotion. "And when I'm not here, I miss Nessie, too." She finally focused on Martin. "And you know how much I love flowers."

Everyone chuckled, except Martin who longed to hear her say the words.

"But what I'd love more than flowers is to be your wife."

Martin rose from his knees and drew her into his arms, his lips touching hers with a gentle kiss. Later when they were alone, he would kiss her with all the love in his heart.

He opened his hand and placed the box on her palm. "It's taken us what seems like a lifetime to meet, but now we'll have a new lifetime together. I love you, Emily."

No sound came from her mouth, but he watched her lips saying "I love you."

He motioned toward the box, urging her to open it. She hadn't expected a ring today. Emily knew his intentions since the day they'd talked, but he'd waited for this special day to share it with the family.

Emily lifted the lid as a hush fell over the family. She

gazed at the ring and then at Martin. "It's breathtaking." Tears clung to her lashes, while a couple broke away and strayed down her cheeks.

"These are happy tears," she said, lifting the ring from the velvet box.

Martin took it and slipped it on her finger, watching the diamond glint in the late afternoon light.

She gazed at the ring, turning her hand in one direction then the other, and finally she lifted her gaze to his and he heard the words. "I love you, Martin, with all my heart."

A bustle of noise followed, everyone talking at the same time. His mother approached them first to look at the ring. "Emily, I've never had a daughter of my own, but God has given me two lovely ones as wives to my sons, and I thank Him." She gazed over her shoulder at Steph, and then at Emily. "But I want you to know that the sparkle in this ring doesn't hold a candle to the light you bring to my life. I'm thrilled to call you daughter."

The tears Emily had tried to control gave way. Martin drew her to his side as the others gathered round in his mother's new sitting room. The joy in his heart went far beyond anything he could have dared ask or dream. He lifted his eyes to Heaven, knowing God's power had been working on him a long time.

# Chapter Sixteen

*Three months later*

Emily lay on the balcony of her honeymoon suite, feeling the sun warming her body and happiness warming her heart. Her diamond glinted in the light, sending prisms of color into the air. The sun, though still warm, had lowered on the horizon where hints of coral and gold spread across the water. Through the sliding glass door of the luxury liner, she heard Martin inside, slipping into his clothes for dinner. A smile curved her lips, picturing her handsome husband dressed in a suit and tie, his eyes only on her and hers only on him.

Martin had opened his heart and she'd followed. She'd lived for years weighted by the pain of her past, and God had made it so simple. Just let go. She'd heard it in church and read it in the Bible, but she'd been unable to release the dismal memories until Martin touched her life. Witnessing his trust and honesty, a struggle for him, too, she'd taken a giant step, and Martin hadn't disappointed her. God hadn't either. He'd provided far more than she could have ever dreamed.

Their wedding day four days earlier still hung in her mind like a beautiful movie. Surrounded by Martin's family, they'd stood with the huge stone fireplace as their backdrop and spoken the promises that would last forever. All doubt had faded from her mind the day Martin listened to her story and loved her anyway. Little by little, she was learning to love herself.

The pastor's words touched her when he read the words from First Corinthians 13. *Love is patient, love is kind. It does not envy, it does not boast, it is not proud. It is not rude, it is not self-seeking, it is not easily angered, it keeps no record of wrongs. Love does not delight in evil but rejoices with the truth. It always protects, always trusts, always hopes, always perseveres.* The verses wrapped around her like a shield from the world. Martin loved her. She loved him, and nothing could harm them now. They'd been honest, and they trusted each other with the darkness of their past. Then the light of love became their beacon. God's love and their own.

Moisture filled Emily's eyes when she thought of Martin's turnaround. When they'd met, she considered him a challenge, but little by little, the true man emerged with all his thoughtfulness and gentle ways. When they'd planned their simple wedding, Martin had insisted she try to locate her sister. Though the plan had failed, Emily's hope had grown. She wouldn't give up. One day they could meet again. She brushed the tears from her eyes, uplifted by the love that the Lord had put in her life.

Despite her sister not being there, the joy Martin's family offered her on their wedding day and even more the love they poured on her every day had wiped away her self-doubts and most of all her fear. Molly and Brent had attended the wedding, too, and even Dee who'd become a big help at the shelter. Julia sat with Mike, their friendship growing, and their smiles lit the room. Julia's matchmaking days had ended, and she'd taken Emily into her heart, giving her the family Emily had always wanted.

A smile curved her lips when she pictured the lovely two-tiered cake with the traditional bride and groom along with a small dog on top. Nessie had been the one who'd brought them together, and she'd become part of the family.

With Nessie in her thoughts, the cake cutting played in her mind, and a chuckle bubbled from her throat as the door slid open. Martin stepped onto the balcony bringing with him the scent of his familiar aftershave.

"You're laughing, and you're alone." His grin flashed at her as he sat at the round glass-topped table.

"I was thinking of Nessie when you dropped the piece of wedding cake you were supposed to feed me, and she ate it. It was kind of appropriate."

He laughed with her. "Mom tried to be a matchmaker for years, but Nessie did the job."

"Martin, thank you for giving me my dream. Every time I saw photographs of the Caribbean with its peacock blue water and golden sand, I longed to have a chance to sink my feet into it. You gave me my dream, and you've opened a new world to me."

"This is new for both of us. I would have drowned in my loneliness. Now I'm a new man."

Tears blurred her eyes as she wondered at the Lord's blessings. Without Him, she couldn't have survived.

Martin leaned closer and kissed the tip of her nose, then lowered his mouth to her lips. Her heart fluttered as it did the first day he'd kissed her, the day he'd noticed her scars. They'd both been surprised by the kiss, but it was the day everything changed. Martin had followed his heart and so had she.

When he drew back, Martin brushed the tears from her lashes before he rose and kissed her eyes.

"You look handsome as always." She drew in a deep breath and slid her legs from the lounge chair. "I suppose I'd better dress for dinner, too."

He grinned. "I think they have rules about dining in your bathing suit."

She stood, but as she did, her gaze settled on the view in front of her. "They're giving us another look at the pinnacles." She moved to the ship's rail, looking ahead at the sparkling shades of turquoise and the twin peaks of the Piton Mountains of Saint Lucia. "That's one of the most beautiful sights I've ever seen."

Martin put his arm around her shoulders. "I've seen much lovelier sights."

"Well, you've traveled all over the world." She looked into his eyes and caught a glint of playfulness.

"No, it's right here." He brushed his hand along her hair, his fingers ruffling the strands, then making their way to her lips. "You are far more lovely than any sight on earth."

Her knees weakened looking into his eyes and she wondered if she would spend a lifetime falling in love over and over every day.

Martin stood behind her, his arms around her body, holding her against his chest and placing kisses on her hair. "You smell like sunshine. I love you, Emily."

She tilted her head to look at him, awed by the gift God had given her. He lit up her world, but the Lord had been their light and their salvation. He had guided their paths and they'd found each other. "I love you."

He turned her toward him, and when he looked into

her eyes, the pinnacles couldn't compete with the beauty she witnessed there. His lips drew closer, as his "Amen" whispered past her and his mouth met hers.

Amen. The perfect prayer.

\* \* \* \* \*

*A Recipe From Gail Gaymer Martin*

If Emily could learn to make this dish, anyone can learn. It's delicious and can be made healthy with low fat cheese and ham.

*Julia's Chicken Cordon Bleu*

2 chicken breasts boned and skinned
2 1-oz. slices of Swiss cheese
2 1-oz. slices of ham
2 tbsp flour
1 well-beaten egg or egg white
½ cup breadcrumbs

Flatten the chicken breasts to $1/8$ inch thick. Cut cheese and ham into strips. Lay the strips of ham and cheese on each chicken breast. Roll breast into cylinder making sure to seal the edges as secure as possible. Wrap and freeze for 15 minutes. Then, dip meat into flour, egg and crumbs. Brown in butter (or a low fat butter substitute). Bake 375° for 15 to 20 minutes until golden.

Option: A white sauce with or without cheese can be drizzled over the chicken dish, but for low fat avoid the sauce or use low fat yogurt mixed with your favorite herbs.

Dear Reader,

I hope you enjoyed *Bride In Training* as well as Molly's and Steph's stories in the first two books of the MAN'S BEST FRIEND series. I've enjoyed owning dogs so these novels came from my heart. Dogs provide their owners unconditional love and faithfulness, which is something we strive for in our own personal relationships. As Emily struggled with the sins of her past, many of us cling to our sins and bad judgments, and we cannot see the light behind the darkness. Emily took a long time to learn that once she released the blackness of her life, the glow of God's love opened doors to other joys. Hope, trust and faith are the keys, and we know the greatest gift is love. This series was written in memory of our daughter, Brenda. After her death, we learned she had helped a woman through the dark moments of considering suicide. The woman accepted Brenda's optimism with blind faith and now lives a fulfilled life. What a blessing God gives us when He provides us opportunities to touch others with love and with hope.

*Gail Gaymer Martin*

QUESTIONS FOR DISCUSSION

1. Did Martin or Emily have to change the most? In what way did the person change? What were the signs that illustrated the change? How did you relate to those changes?

2. Forgiving oneself is a theme that runs through this book and the other two in the series. Have you ever had difficulty forgiving yourself for something? How is this made more complex by being a Christian?

3. Flowers provided a metaphor in this story. Julia made references to this when arranging flowers in the vase, and flowers also represented something important to Emily. What was it?

4. Why did flowers around a home mean so much to Emily? Contrast this to her past life.

5. Martin commented many times on Emily's oversize clothing. Was this important to the plot, and if so what did it mean? When did Emily begin to wear clothes that fit her?

6. Both characters were believers. Did you see any difference in their expression of faith? How did their faith affect their lives?

7. One theme of this novel could be found in the Bible verse quoted in the front of the book from *Ephesians* 3:20: "By His mighty power at work within us, He

is able to accomplish infinitely more than we would ever dare to ask or hope." Explain this theme and how it worked in the novel.

8. Emily could not see her worthiness. She believed the only talent she had was training dogs. What attributes and talents did you notice in Emily that she didn't see? Do you think people often do not recognize their own abilities and attributes?

9. Emily's crooked tooth brought on the discussion of making "a mountain out of a molehill." Do you know anyone who does this? How does this affect our lives? Can you think of something in your own life that seems a "mountain" when others don't see it that way?

10. Have you ever owned a pet? Pets do offer unconditional love, but we know they are work, too. Did any of the incidents in this novel remind you of humorous or difficult experiences in your life that relate to pets?

11. How important is trust in a relationship? Have you ever acted in a way that you were ashamed? How did that affect your life? Steph and Emily expressed different viewpoints about being honest about their pasts with their partners. Who do you agree with?

12. Loneliness is another theme in this novel. Martin was lonely and so was Julia. Have you experienced this kind of loneliness? What can a person do to change those feelings?

# TITLES AVAILABLE NEXT MONTH

## Available July 27, 2010

**THE DOCTOR'S BLESSING**
*Brides of Amish Country*
**Patricia Davids**

**TREASURE CREEK DAD**
*Alaskan Bride Rush*
**Terri Reed**

**HOMETOWN PROPOSAL**
*Kellerville*
**Merrillee Whren**

**THE COWBOY'S SWEETHEART**
**Brenda Minton**

**HOMECOMING HERO**
**Renee Ryan**

**WEDDING CAKE WISHES**
*Wedding Bell Blessings*
**Dana Corbit**

# LARGER-PRINT BOOKS!

## GET 2 FREE
## LARGER-PRINT NOVELS
## PLUS 2 FREE
## MYSTERY GIFTS

### Larger-print novels are now available...

**YES!** Please send me 2 FREE LARGER-PRINT Love Inspired® novels and my 2 FREE mystery gifts (gifts are worth about $10). After receiving them, if I don't wish to receive any more books, I can return the shipping statement marked "cancel". If I don't cancel, I will receive 6 brand-new novels every month and be billed just $4.74 per book in the U.S. or $5.24 per book in Canada. That's a saving of over 20% off the cover price. It's quite a bargain! Shipping and handling is just 50¢ per book.* I understand that accepting the 2 free books and gifts places me under no obligation to buy anything. I can always return a shipment and cancel at any time. Even if I never buy another book, the two free books and gifts are mine to keep forever.

122/322 IDN E7QP

Name                                        (PLEASE PRINT)

Address                                                                             Apt. #

City                          State/Prov.                          Zip/Postal Code

Signature (if under 18, a parent or guardian must sign)

#### Mail to **Steeple Hill Reader Service:**
**IN U.S.A.:** P.O. Box 1867, Buffalo, NY 14240-1867
**IN CANADA:** P.O. Box 609, Fort Erie, Ontario L2A 5X3

Not valid to current subscribers to Love Inspired Larger-Print books.

**Are you a current subscriber to Love Inspired books
and want to receive the larger-print edition?
Call 1-800-873-8635 or visit www.morefreebooks.com.**

* Terms and prices subject to change without notice. Prices do not include applicable taxes. Sales tax applicable in N.Y. Canadian residents will be charged applicable provincial taxes and GST. Offer not valid in Quebec. This offer is limited to one order per household. All orders subject to approval. Credit or debit balances in a customer's account(s) may be offset by any other outstanding balance owed by or to the customer. Please allow 4 to 6 weeks for delivery. Offer available while quantities last.

**Your Privacy:** Steeple Hill Books is committed to protecting your privacy. Our Privacy Policy is available online at www.SteepleHill.com or upon request from the Reader Service. From time to time we make our lists of customers available to reputable third parties who may have a product or service of interest to you. If you would prefer we not share your name and address, please check here. ☐

**Help us get it right**—We strive for accurate, respectful and relevant communications. To clarify or modify your communication preferences, visit us at www.ReaderService.com/consumerschoice.

LILP10R

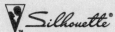
# ROMANTIC
# *SUSPENSE*

**Sparked by Danger, Fueled by Passion.**

SILHOUETTE ROMANTIC SUSPENSE BRINGS YOU
AN ALL-NEW COLTONS OF MONTANA STORY!

THE COLTONS
-OF MONTANA-

FBI agent Jake Pierson is determined to solve his case,
even if it means courting and using the daughter of a
murdered informant. Mary Walsh hates liars and,
now that Jake has fallen deeply in love, he is afraid
to tell her the truth. But the truth is not the only
thing out there to hurt Mary...

Be part of the romance and suspense in

*Covert Agent's Virgin Affair*

by
# LINDA CONRAD

*Available August 2010 where books are sold.*

**Visit Silhouette Books at www.eHarlequin.com**

SRS27690